A Name with No Meaning

By Patrick Madden

"A Name with No Meaning," by Pat Madden. ISBN 978-1-951985-99-8.

Published 2021 by Virtualbookworm.com Publishing Inc., P.O. Box 9949, College Station, TX 77842, US. ©2013, Pat Madden. All rights reserved. No part of this publication may be reproduced, stored in a retrieval system, or transmitted in any form or by any means, electronic, mechanical, recording or otherwise, without the prior written permission of Pat Madden.

I am a Welshman born in a little mining town called Blaenavon. My Mother was Welsh and my Father Irish. I grew up spending most of my time playing in local woods, making rope swings and building stone cabins with rusty corrugated sheets for a roof, not studying as I should have. After marrying and living life to the full I am now retired. I had five children and love them all dearly.

I was inspired to write this story one day as I was collecting logs from a quiet peaceful forest near my home. I was thinking about my daughter and what she had said to me. She was very concerned about children not being baptized. As I walked along I thought I would write a fairy story about her concerns in the hope of enlightening children and their parents.

Since writing this story in 2004, sadly my darling daughter Julie passed away on Valentine's Day 2006. I dedicate this story to her memory.

$\mathcal{O}ne$

In the wonderful world of Fairyland, there lives a Fairy Queen; her name is Roaniler. She's married to Drahol, the most powerful King of Fairies ever known, and they live together in Vanbolena Castle. Vanbolena is the capital city of Fairyland, and its castle is the tallest of all, reaching high above the city. In Vanbolena, every twenty-five years, during the full moon in May, an exciting event happens. At midnight, the Queen flies from the Tower of Life, down the enchanted moonbeams, to the land of Gormethoda. There she will give birth to her Royal baby.

All young fairies live like any other child; going to school, playing, etc. They are born gifted with intelligence and the ability to communicate. Fairies look just like us, but their bone structure is as light and delicate as a bird. They weigh no more than two stone and can grow up to five feet tall, but with magic, can be small enough to fly through keyholes. It only takes a wave of their wand, and they are invisible to the human eye. Once they reach the age of sixteen, they can fall in love, marry and live for two hundred years or even more.

Now, whether you know this or not, Royal Fairies are the only fairies born without wings. They receive them by their Fairy Godmother's magic, one hour after they are born. Royal fairy wings are very special; they are enchanted. This enables them to fly extremely fast, even through water. These lovely wings are a beautiful, ice blue colour, and as they fly through the moonbeams during the night of a full moon, they flash with all the colours of a rainbow. Three hours after a Royal child is born, the bells of Gormethoda will ring out, signalling the Queen to fly with her child back home to Vanbolena. She will fly through the very same beams she came down on, only this time, halfway to Vanbolena, is the Royal River of Diamond Crystals. This mystic Royal River only appears once in every twenty-five years. It is a river formed by millions upon millions of tiny floating purple crystals. In this spectacular display of soft, beautiful rays, is where every fairy receives a silver wand with a twinkling star on its tip. Each little star is a twinkle, taken from Venus, the brightest star in the universe and every twinkle's unique. All fairies need a wand, but only after reaching the age of sixteen does the magic begin to flow through it. Before entering the Royal River, a tiny skylark named Calandra will reveal their names. Every name has a special meaning. This meaning will be made known to them by a white dove inside the river. Without this special meaning, fairies will have no magical powers, never be happy in love, unable to marry and will stay that way, miserable forever.

Only the Queen and her new-born child can pass through the Royal River of purple crystals. Other mothers and their children also pass through this river, but for their ceremony, the floating crystals are sparkling yellow.

Now that you have some idea of what is about to happen, I'll get on with the story.

It was now the magic month of May in the year of the quarter-century. The moon was full, and with the midnight hour approaching, every fairy in Fairyland was singing and dancing with excitement. Their beloved Queen was now preparing herself for the long journey down the silvery beams of the moon. The Queen was dressed in beautiful midnight blue, and around her shoulders delicately lay a white shawl with long golden frills. This lovely shawl was pinned safely with a brooch of gold, covered with glistening blue sapphires. Around her shining hazel hair came dazzling rays of light radiated from a glorious crown full of diamonds. Her dainty midnight blue shoes were also dotted with the same beautiful jewels that glistened like snow in the moonlight.

Queen Roaniler, all dressed and well prepared, kissed her beloved husband and said, "I am ready."

The kind-hearted King smiled, held her in his arms, kissed her and said, "I love you."

The king then went out onto the balcony overlooking his kingdom and stretched out his arms. With a clear voice, he announced to a million cheering fairies that their lovely Queen was beginning to make her way to the enchanted Tower of Life.

The radiant Queen rode through the streets in a gleaming silver carriage drawn by twelve jet black horses with silver studded harnesses and solid silver shoes. Unattached and leading this shining team was a magnificent palomino stallion, gently swishing his long white tail. His wavy white mane seemed to ripple as he moved his proud head from side to side. The Queen's carriage was flanked by ten Royal Guards, five on each side. Their tunics were midnight blue with gold threads made by the only gold spinning spider in the world. Their sandals were made of leather with laces neatly crisscrossed up to their knees. At the rear were two more Royal Guards dressed exactly the same. So too was the coach fairy, driving the royal team. The guards, as they marched along, proudly carried their wands across their chest. It was a glorious sight, and as this long-awaited procession made its way through the streets, excited fairies lined the route, cheering and singing praises to their lovely Queen. The very moment the royal carriage stopped at the bottom of the steps leading up to the tower, the magnificent palomino reared up onto his hind legs and whinnied out a cry that was heard all over Fairyland.

There are three hundred steps leading up to the Tower of Life, and every step represents a month in a quarter of a century. On top of the tower stands the large Balance Arch, made of unbreakable, coloured stained glass. At the stroke of midnight, it is through this spectacular arch that the warm, full moonbeams will flow. These very special beams will enable the Queen to fly on her exciting journey down its silvery enchanted path to the land of Gormethoda. Inside, and hanging down from the roof of this arch, is the Great Bell of Wonder. The bell was hand-carved from precious metal taken from Coity Mountain, the coldest mountain in the world of fairies. On the rear of this marvellous bell sits a jewel called a Blism, the only one of its kind.

The Queen, accompanied by her Royal Guards, had climbed the steps to the top of the tower and was now patiently waiting in the middle of the glass arch. With her outstretched wings quivering gently in the breeze, the moon slowly began to fill the arch with its soft enchanting beams. At the stroke of midnight, just as these magic beams made contact with the sacred Blism, a spiralling rainbow was sent at great speed back into the moon. At that moment, the great Bell of Wonder rang out as the moon filled the arch showering the beautiful Queen with its endless silvery beams. Roaniler smiled and as she looked back at the moon, raised her arms and flew away alone as every bell in Fairyland rang out with joy.

As the Queen flew away, there was a mighty flash way above the stars. The moon was now being held still by some unknown powerful magic. This enabled the moon to stay beaming through the lovely glass arch. The magic holding the moon lasts for three hours only. On the stroke of that third hour, the Queen must make her way back with her child, or they will be lost forever.

The beams led the Queen to Capel Newydd Castle, standing high on a hill in the land of Gormethoda. Rathier, the Fairy Godmother, lives in this castle and will look after Roaniler and her new-born child until the hour of three o'clock.

When Queen Roaniler arrived at Gormethoda, she flew into her room at the top of Capel Newydd Castle. Greeting her was Rathier, the Fairy Godmother. Rathier lovingly smiled and showed the Queen to her royal bed, telling her to rest awhile and not to worry. Roaniler lay down and tried to relax but soon became very anxious for she knew that time was precious. Rathier stayed at the Queen's bedside, comforting her until the child was to be born.

When that time came, the fairy godmother, with her wand raised high above her head, conjured up and cried out special magic words. Suddenly, a stream of magic from her sparkling wand surrounded the lovely Queen with a coloured mist, completely covering her from view. Instantaneously, flying out from this soft coloured mist, flew a little bird that circled once then flew away. With another wave of Rathier's wand, the cloud of magic disappeared, leaving two lovely little fairy girls. The two little girls were sitting on the bed beside their mother, both holding a tiny green crystal in their hand. The fairy godmother took the two crystals and put them away in an old jewellery box. These little crystals are called a Trish. It is the small part of a special emerald broken in two the moment they were born. All fairies are born with these in their hands.

Queen Roaniler was now the proud mother of twins. She was surprised and cuddled her princesses close to her.

"You must bathe them now, my Queen," said the fairy godmother after fetching and bringing in a bath

Roaniler began to gently wash them in a bath of warmed spring water from the famous Nanny Goats Spout. The Nanny Goats Spout is a special everlasting spring that runs out from Vanbolena Mountain, guarded by Keepers. After they had been bathed and dried, the Queen wrapped them in two pink shawls to keep them warm. She then lay them on her bed and smiled lovingly, with both princesses smiling back. At that moment, the Queen noticed that one of her princesses was amazingly beautiful. This stunned the Queen into sighs of amazement until she eventually lay alongside the twins and fell asleep.

At the hour of two o'clock, it was time for the princesses to receive their wings. Rathier gently woke the Queen from her sleep. The little royals were already awake and as Rathier began to unravel them from their shawls, she was also amazed by what she saw. One of the princesses was stunningly beautiful, like no one she had ever seen. The Queen, once again, gasped in wonder, but they had no time to lose. The Royal family had to be on their way before it was too late. Rathier asked the princesses to go inside a circle of small, coloured, fluttering butterflies. They were to sit down with their legs crossed and their arms folded. The fairy godmother then raised and pointed her wand three times towards them. The butterflies now began to fly at high speed around the two little royal heads showering them with all their lovely colours, shedding from their wings. Their colours formed a beautiful coloured mist, completely covering the little princesses for exactly one minute. With another three waves from Rathier's wand, the butterflies settled back down, still fluttering their wings, only this time they were snowy white. Rathier, after waving her wand once more, the coloured cloud surrounding the princesses slowly drifted back onto the wings of the butterflies, giving them back their lovely colours.

Hovering now, were two delighted princesses, two feet tall and both looking up at their beautiful fluttering wings. They quickly flew over to the Queen, kissed her gently on the cheek, and said, "Hello, Mother."

"Hello, my little ones," said their mother, as she gently hugged them. "Come, we must hurry!"

The Queen dressed the twins in white, but no shoes were to be worn while passing through the River of Diamond Crystals. The twins looked so lovely and as they hovered alongside the Queen, they waited patiently for their fairy godmother, who had since left the room.

As we know, when the twins were born, their emeralds were broken into two pieces, one larger than the other. The larger of the two, called a Cened, contains the fairy's name. The smaller piece called a Trish holds the meaning to their name.

The fairy godmother soon returned and opened up the old jewellery box. She took out the two little crystal Trishes that she had taken from the twins earlier and said as she placed them into each of their hands.

7

"On your journey up through the moonbeams, you will meet a little skylark, named Calandra. The moment all fairies are born, Calandra collects and takes their precious Cened to a sacred font inside a Royal River of Diamond Crystals. At the entrance to this river is where Calandra will be waiting to let you know your names. Once known, Calandra will open the gates allowing you to enter the river. As you do so, you will see your wands lying on two crystal waves. Following their collection, you must fly and place your little Trish, which I have now given you, into the sacred font situated in the middle of the river. Inside this font, lying in icy cold liquid will be your Cened. The Cened will then be reunited with your Trish, enabling you to know the meaning of your name and the true meaning of the emerald."

Rathier smiled, kissed them and turning to the delighted Queen she said, "Your, Highness. The lovely princesses are now ready."

With it now almost three o'clock, Rathier opened the Queen's bedroom window to reveal the bright full moon and its beams. Roaniler and her princesses stood in the middle of the beams and waited. Then, just as the clock on the castle tower chimed three times, the unknown magic faded, releasing the full moon from its power. The Queen and her princesses opened up their wings and flew away to the sound of every bell in Gormethoda.

The night was warm and all the stars were twinkling brightly. Queen Roaniler and her children enjoyed the view and could still hear the bells of Gormethoda behind them. They were all very excited, more so were the princesses because they had never seen the world before. As they made their way up and up the dancing moonbeams, they raced one another. The

Queen laughed and let them win, pretending that they were too fast for her.

After seeing a bright glistening glow above, the royal twins began to feel very nervous and held their mother's hands. Approaching this light, the twins saw a beautiful singing skylark. He was hovering in front of a dazzling emerald green gate, covered in sparkling diamonds. The Queen stopped in front of the skylark and bowed her head. The princesses did the same.

"Welcome, Queen Roaniler," said the skylark in a soft, kind voice. "You may raise your head."

The Queen raised her head and said to the skylark, "I bring my newborn princesses for their sacred ceremony. We await your announcement of their names."

The princesses, still with their heads bowed, were standing on each side of their mother. The skylark plucked a small feather from underneath its wing and placed it on the head of the princess standing on the right side of the Queen and said, "Your name is Anoralee."

Princess Anoralee was pleased, thanked the skylark and smiled.

The skylark now turned to the second princess, plucked a feather from underneath its other wing, and placed it on her head, saying, "Your name is Tianaju."

Princess Tianaju was also very pleased, raised her head, looked at Calandra, thanked him and smiled. At that moment, the skylark flew back, startled by the incredible beauty of the princess. She was the most beautiful fairy he had ever seen. Queen Roaniler noticed how surprised the bird was and knew just what he was thinking, for she could not believe it herself. Calandra settled down again but was still in awe of the princess's beauty. He then stretched out his wings and soared up into the air, singing a song. His song opened up the illuminated gates, and the royal family entered the river.

They flew into a wonderful sight of floating, sparkling crystals that were softer than the softest snowflakes. On the crest of two crystal waves, were their wands, each one bore their name. The little princesses flew up and nervously collected them. Roaniler comforted them with a little cuddle.

"I am really proud of you, but now my children, with very little time left, we must go on to complete the ceremony."

All three quickly flew onwards to the middle of the river where the most important and vital stage of their life was in sight. In front of them now was a sparkling font. Queen Roaniler flew with her very nervous daughters up to the sacred font. She smiled then asked Anoralee to place her little Trish inside. So, Princess Anoralee, while holding the crystal in her outstretched hand, placed it into the font that was half-full of an extremely cold liquid. At that moment, rising out of the font came a quivering pure white dove. It hovered above Anoralee's head for a moment, then disappeared back into the font. The princess now knew the meaning of her name. She was so excited that she shouted out with joy, did a few little spins, flew off up the moonbeams and back again. The Queen and Tianaju watched her race and laughed as she did a little jig.

Roaniler turned now and looked at Tianaju, smiled, and said, "It's your turn now."

The beautiful princess flew towards the font with her arm outstretched, holding the tiny Trish in her hand. Suddenly, there was a blinding flash and a hand of fire snatched the crystal away from the astonished princess, leaving a small burn mark in the palm of her hand. The Queen quickly waved her wand to try and stop the flaming hand, but it was too late; it had vanished. Poor Tianaju was in distress and with tears rolling down her beautiful face, she asked the Queen,

"Oh, my hand! What happened, Mother? Where's my little crystal Trish gone?"

The Queen didn't know what had happened, but it was getting late and time to fly.

"Nothing like this has ever happened before," she replied. "But hurry now my little ones, for we are late. The moon will be halfway across the emerald arch by now. So, fly my princesses, for without the moonbeams, we will never get back to Vanbolena. Don't worry, Tianaju; your father will know what to do."

The Royal family flew away and arrived at the Emerald Arch just before the last centre moonbeam faded.

"My children say nothing to anyone about what happened at the river. Everything will be fine once we speak to your father," said the Queen.

Royal Guards were waiting at the Emerald Arch to accompany their Queen and her princesses down the long three hundred steps and into the royal carriage below. As the Royal family made their way down and into their golden carriage, every bell in Fairyland rang out for joy, and every fairy cheered with excitement.

"Congratulations! We love you, your Majesty," shouted all the fairies as the carriage passed on through the city.

The King was pleased to see the Queen arrive and was very surprised to find that he was now a father of twins. Both princesses flew up to the King, kissed him, and said, "Hello Father!"

"Hello, my little princesses," said Drahol as he gave them a big hug.

Almost immediately, the King noticed how beautiful Tianaju was but didn't mention it. He then asked them their names.

"Oh, they are lovely names, my children," said the King with delight. "Now you can tell me their meanings?"

Before the King could say another word, the Queen spoke out.

"I have something to tell you, Drahol. Something that cannot wait.

The Queen rang a bell, and in came excited maids to take the princesses to their rooms. The King wondered, but waited until his daughters had left before asking the Queen.

"What you are going to tell me, has it anything to do with Tianaju being so very beautiful?"

"Yes, it does happen to be Tianaju," replied the Queen. "But no, Drahol, it isn't because she is so beautiful. It's something very serious."

The Queen sat down and told the very curious King exactly what had happened.

Meanwhile, except for one young boy fairy, no one had noticed a shadow on the moon. This fairy always liked looking at the moon, especially when it was full. So, after witnessing the shadow, he called out, "Look! There's a shadow on the moon!"

Those who heard the boy, all looked up, and sure enough, there was a small black shadow on the upper left-hand side of the moon. The word went around very quickly, and soon, everyone was talking about it. Then, without warning and with no clouds in the sky, it began to rain. The rain lasted for five minutes, but not a single fairy got wet

"Look? The moon is weeping. How can this be?" cried an elderly fairy.

Some said this, others said that, but no one knew the proper answer to why there was a strange-looking shadow on the pure white moon.

Meanwhile, back in the castle, an anxious and baffled King had no answer for his distraught wife.

"I have no idea how such a terrible thing could have happened to Tianaju. It is impossible. No one is allowed inside the River of Diamond Crystals."

The King and Queen then decided to look in the only two books concerning the Royal River. They collected the books from their huge library and sat down to read them. Unfortunately, they found nothing that would help solve this frustrating mystery. Next, they summoned up all their powers of knowledge, even counted all the stars, checking to see if maybe one had fallen and knocked the crystal out of the princess's hand. But no, all the stars were still there. After searching all through the night, a very distraught King and Queen sat down on their thrones.

"Ah, it's no use; the crystal is gone forever," sighed Drahol. "Poor, little, beautiful Tianaju. I cannot help her, but no one must know this, my dear. They will know soon enough on her sixteenth birthday. Until then, we must do everything possible to find this violating thief and why he stole the crystal. Maybe then, and only then, will we be able to retrieve the stolen Trish, even if it's at a price."

The twins were up early in the morning and were now sitting around the breakfast table enjoying a nice bowl of porridge with their parents. The King had read the morning newspapers and was mystified learning about the dark shadow and how it poured with rain without anyone getting wet.

"Very strange," said Drahol to the Queen. "I wonder what causes this shadow."

"We'll take a look tonight, my love, while the children are asleep," replied the Queen.

So that evening, before the twins went to bed, the King told Tianaju not to worry about what had happened

13

to her at the font. He intended to seek out its cause and would do his utmost to get her little Trish back. Although disappointed, the princess had faith in her father and went to bed, happy enough with her sister. By this time, the moon was out in full. King Drahol and Roaniler were on top of their tall castle looking at what everyone was talking about. They were astonished, for sure enough there was a small black shadow on the upper left-hand side of the pure white moon. The King studied it for a while until he gasped in horror.

"Oh, no!" Said the King, staggering back. "This must have something to do with what happened to Tianaju. Whoever snatched the crystal away from her has far greater power than I. The shadow you see is not a shadow; it is a black mountain in the shape of a clenched hand."

The King knew this because he is the only fairy able to see that far. Roaniler was so upset upon hearing this; she flew down to Tianaju's bedroom in tears.

Drahol stood there staring at the moon, deep in thought muttering to himself.

"What is the meaning of this? Why has this happened to my daughter?"

The mystified King paced around for a while before flying down alongside the Queen. Tianaju was now fast asleep, and as they stood by her bedside, the King said as he took Roaniler's hand.

"She is so beautiful, and to have this very sad life before her, breaks my heart? But we'll leave her now and talk more in the morning."

All through that special month of May life went on as usual. Nothing else out of the ordinary happened. The shadow was still there, disappearing only after the last quarter moon.

June soon came around, but for five nights before the full moon, a strange cloud appeared, completely covering the moon from view. When the night of the full moon finally came, there were many nervous fairies. All waiting in anticipation, asking one another all kinds of questions.

"Will the shadow still be there? I hope the cloud has gone. Do you think the moon is going to fall apart? What if it goes out?"

They were all looking towards the east, and as the moon slowly began to rise, they held on to each other until it was way above the mountain. The cloud had gone, but to everyone's dismay, the shadow was still there. King Drahol, the Queen, and her princesses were watching from the castle tower. Apart from the shadow, the twins thought the moon looked absolutely lovely.

Roaniler looked at the King, and with both of them shaking their heads, she whispered,

"Life must go on, for nothing, not even our magic, can change what has happened to the moon and Tianaju."

Life went on as normal and like all children, the princesses played tricks, teased and hid from one another. They also studied. Learning all about the world, growing wise in all subjects. Meanwhile, the shadow was still there, no larger, no smaller. It was there for everyone to see, but no one could explain its existence.

On the twins sixteenth birthday, a party was being held at the castle and every royal throughout the land were invited. There was rejoicing in the streets, valleys, dales, hills, trees, and mountains. They were all having a wonderful time celebrating the royal twins coming of age. Being sixteen was a special time in every fairy's life. By now the Princesses were fully grown with Anoralee at the normal height of five feet, but to everyone's amazement, for the first time in the history of fairies, Tianaju had grown to five feet two inches tall.

They were now at the age to fall in love and marry, but best of all, it was the time their wands received their magic. Sadly though, this wasn't to be for Tianaju. So, that evening, just before the princesses' wands were to receive their magic, the King sent for Tianaju to sit with him and the Queen in their summer house. When she arrived, the King sadly told her what he had been dreading for a long time.

"My dear Tianaju, my beautiful, beautiful little princess. Unfortunately, we have been unable to retrieve your crystal. Without knowing the meaning to your name, your wand will have no magical powers. You can never be happy in love, and never ever be able to marry. I am so sorry my dear daughter, but without the crystal, I cannot foresee what will happen to you in the future."

The princess ran to her bedroom crying, leaving her parents distraught.

After that terrible night, she stayed in the castle, not venturing out for twelve long months. Poor Tianaju cried and cried every single day, tormented by the thoughts of what she was going to do with the rest of her life. How could she live without being loved? The princess was stunningly beautiful, so never to be loved and married would be heart-breaking for her. She thought it extremely unfair because her poor little heart had been ready for love for some time.

Two

On the twins' seventeenth birthday, King Drahol announced the sad news of what had happened to the poor princess and how it was beyond his power to help her. Every fairy in the land had wondered why Tianaju was so sad and wouldn't come out with her sister. On hearing this, they rallied together and promised to support her always. This made the pretty little princess feel much better. So, she began to enjoy life once more, going out, helping fairies in their work, playing sports and going dancing with her sister. The beautiful princess loved dancing and did as often as she could, even on her own in her bedroom at night. All the young male fairies would take turns dancing with her, but as time went by, all grew afraid of falling in love with the princess. As you can imagine, it was very difficult not to fall in love with someone so beautiful. No one wanted to fall in love with Tianaju, not just for their sake, but also for Tianaju's. They all knew very well that they could never marry her.

Then one afternoon in November, while walking through the woodland of Gingers, Princess Anoralee and Tianaju met a well-dressed young man. He looked very much like a prince or someone very rich. He was sitting on a log peeling one of a few apples he had in his pocket.

"Hello there," said the stranger, who stood up and bowed. "Would I be right in saying that I have been so lucky in meeting two lovely princesses?"

The twins were startled and couldn't figure out how he knew they were princesses, for neither wore tiaras.

"You are right, Sir," replied Anoralee. "Who are you, and what are you doing here?"

"My name is Etredelmah. I have come here bearing a message from Nuraleth."

Anoralee, being the most inquisitive of the princesses, asked the stranger.

"Would this message be something exciting, and could we ask who it is for?"

"The message is not at all exciting, Princess," replied Etredelmah solemnly. "It concerns a mission of high importance, a life-threatening assignment. One I do not envy."

"Oh!" gasped the princesses.

"Ah, no more about that," said Etredelmah. "But I'd be grateful if you could stay and talk awhile. Tell me all about life here in Vanbolena."

The two sisters found the stranger friendly and also very handsome. So they agreed, sat down, and talked for nearly two hours.

It was now four o'clock, and the sun was going down. The princesses were ready to go home, but before they left, Tianaju asked Etredelmah.

"Where do you live, and will we ever see you again, for we did so enjoy our little chat?"

"I live near a place called Hetraleonie, and yes, we will probably meet again one day," he replied. "I too enjoyed our little chat and only wish I could repay you, but I have nothing, only a message."

Anoralee laughed and said, "Well, we don't want that. One of your apples will do nicely."

"Fair enough," replied Etredelmah. "I had forgotten about those. Take your pick."

The princesses took one each and said thank you and goodbye to their new friend.

The two sisters flew home giggling and talking about their newfound friend.

"Do you think we will ever see him again, Anoralee?" asked Tianaju.

"I hope so," replied her sister. "He's so handsome and friendly too, isn't he?"

Arriving home, they went to their rooms to wash and change for dinner. Before going down to the dining room, Princess Tianaju took a bite from her apple and found something inside. It was a green ribbon with a strange kind of message written on it, in very small writing.

'Climb mountain with purpose before it's too late.
This shadow must fall, or you'll enter no gate.
Then, tell other shadows what you've been shown.
So they too will be happy and have what I own.'

"What kind of message is this? Is it the message Etredelmah was talking about? And why give it to me?" Muttered the beautiful princess.

During dinner, the princesses told their parents all about their afternoon with Etredelmah. When they had finished their meal, Tianaju showed her father the message and told him how she got it. King Drahol thought he knew what most of the message meant, but it puzzled him, regardless.

In the evening, while the princesses were sitting around the living room fire, the King and Queen came in to join them. Drahol sat down on the couch and decided to tell his children that the shadow on the moon was a black mountain in the shape of a clenched hand. He then went on to tell Tianaju that he thought her stolen Trish had been placed somewhere in that mountain by a very powerful source. From the message in her apple, for the poor unfortunate princess to be happy, she had to first free the moon of its shadow by climbing the mountain in search of her crystal. It didn't make sense, but it was all the King could say.

The princess was so excited now. All she ever wanted was to find her crystal so that she could be happy.

"But how? How dear father, can I get to the moon?" asked Tianaju, desperately.

The King replied, but sadly, "I have no knowledge of how this can be achieved, but I promise you, my daughter, if it's ever possible, I'll find out."

Tianaju went to bed that night, dreaming of going to the moon and being happy forever.

Months went by, and during that time, the King searched relentlessly for the stranger, Etredelmah, but, unfortunately, without any success. No one had ever heard of him, and neither did they know of any possible route to the moon. It was hopeless.

"It's impossible," said a wise fairy after searching through his book of knowledge.

Three years went by and the princesses were now twenty years of age. Princess Anoralee had fallen deeply in love and married a prince from Lovernal and lived in Lovernal Castle. Poor Princess Tianaju was now left very lonely. Every time she fell in love with someone, they always left her heartbroken. After seeing the burn mark in the palm of her hand, they all knew she was the marked princess who they could never marry. By now, the broken-hearted princess was so upset and desperate, she decided to leave home to seek her destiny.

So, one sunny day in May, after her twenty-first birthday, Tianaju, with tears rolling down her beautiful face, spoke to the King.

"There is no future for me at all, dear Father. My only hope is to find how I can get to the moon and climb that dreaded mountain. I so much want to be happy. Someone, somewhere out there, must have the answer."

"Go then, my pretty one," said the King. "Your mother and I will be deeply sorry to see you go, but it is the only thing left for you to do. I am so sorry that I could not help you."

That night, Tianaju prepared herself for her mission by setting up a map of Fairyland. The first place to visit was Gingers' woodland. It was there the princess and her sister first met the stranger, Etredelmah.

"Where is he?" she asked herself. "Where does he live? If only I could find him, then perhaps he will tell me how to reach the moon. After all! It was he who gave me this task!"

A few weeks later, on a morning in June, Princess Tianaju, with her pack wrapped around the back of her waist, kissed her mother and father and told them she was leaving. Before she went, her mother told her to be careful and if she ever needed her help at any time, all she had to do was tell the birds. Her father gave her a purse full of gold coins, more than enough to provide her on her journey.

Tianaju had no magical powers, so her wand was useless, plus she was unable to reduce her height like all other fairies. All she could do was fly. So, the princess, after tying the purse to a red silk belt around her waist, kissed and said goodbye to her parents then flew away, waving as she went. The saddened Queen began to cry. Drahol put his arm around her in comfort and watched their lovely daughter fly until out of sight.

"Will she be alright, dear?" asked the weeping Queen.

"She is strong in mind and body, so hopefully, it will help her through," he replied.

So, Tianaju, after landing in the woodland of Gingers, made her way to where she first met Etredelmah. After finding the very spot, she sat down, deep in thought.

"What do I do now?" she pondered when suddenly, she heard and saw a very happy looking elf strolling along swinging a stick.

"Oh, hello there," he said. "Are you waiting for someone, my Lady?"

At that moment, his eyes opened wide in amazement. He was stunned and stood there for a moment in a daze until he joked.

"I hope it's me you are looking for? I have never seen anyone so lovely in all my life."

"I'm Princess Tianaju, and I am not waiting for anyone; in fact, it's the very opposite. I'm looking for someone. Someone by the name of Etredelmah."

The elf sat down and listened to Tianaju's tragic story about her little crystal Trish and the seemingly impossible task given to her by the stranger in these woods.

"Hmm, so that shadow is a mountain on the moon, eh? How are you supposed to get up there?" asked the puzzled elf.

"This is what I am trying to find out and why I need to talk with Etredelmah," replied the princess. "Can you help me?"

The elf, taking his time in answering, agreed, "Okay. Yes, I'll help you. I know an elk that stays not far from here. His name is Bellow. He just might know this stranger and where he lives. Come, I'll take you to him. Oh, by the way, my name is Pheler."

Off they went walking through the woods, chatting together about their lives and likes. On the way, the elf found himself feeling very sorry for the princess. So he made up his mind to help her find someone with the knowledge of how to reach the moon.

They walked on through the forest enjoying themselves exchanging stories until Pheler stopped and pointed. Up on a hill, between the trees was a lovely big chestnut-coloured elk, standing six feet tall to his shoulders. He was handsome, and as they drew closer to him, the elk roared out.

"Whoa, Pheler! And who is this beautiful lady, may I ask? And where are you going?"

Pheler introduced Tianaju then asked the great elk if he would listen to her. Bellow kindly agreed and listened. The princess told the elk everything that had happened then asked if he knew Etredelmah or had he ever heard of him.

"Well now," said the elk looking lovingly at her. "I think I might know this Etredelmah fellow. I've seen him pass this way from time to time, usually in the autumn. You say he came with a message from Nuraleth and that he lives near Hetraleonie. Well, I have never heard of Nuraleth, and Hetraleonie is a long way for you to travel alone, Princess."

"She will not be alone," interrupted Pheler. "I am with her all the way."

The elk continued, "Yes, but there will be unforeseen dangers. This route takes you through lands of greedy, jealous cruel fairies, gnomes and elves. With your looks, Princess, you will surely fall into the wrong hands. Knowing this, I have decided to come with you, but only as far as Iwedilli. So, come now, the pair of you up onto my back, we had better get started. But wait, before we go, Princess, there will be times when you'll have to conceal your wings."

"Yes, my wings can fold up really small under my hair. Shall I do it now?" She asked.

"With you not having magical powers, Princess, it would be better if you did. Many jealous folks would love to damage a fairy's wings."

Tianaju folder her wings neatly under her hair, and away the three went.

Three

ellow trotted steadily on through woods, over many hills and rivers before stopping to eat. There were all kinds of fruit, berries, and vegetation for them all to enjoy. Also, in Fairland, they are lucky enough to have nuts the whole year-round. Tianaju loves them. While they were resting, the elk and Pheler told the princess about some of the adventures they had experienced. There were so many, it was an hour before they raced away out of the woods into the sunshine.

It was early evening before an outline of a town came into view. Bellow slowed down and turned his head to warn his friends.

"We are now approaching the town of Lidapler. The gnomes who live there are very jealous, constantly competing against one another. Each one, trying to be the most important person in the land. They are all very well dressed, and their homes and buildings are spotless."

With that said, the great elk, Tianaju, and Pheler slowly made their way into Lidapler, cautiously looking around them.

The gnomes were busy doing something; if they weren't laughing, they were crying, if they weren't playing, they were fighting, and if they were not talking, they were shouting. You could very well say this is normal behaviour, it probably is, but the only difference was, they all hated one another. Everyone wanted to be better than the next. Lidapler was not a nice place to be. Nevertheless, the companions had to rest, for the sun had gone, and the night was upon them.

They were weary now from travelling, so the elk found a nice spot just outside town, underneath a large wide weeping willow tree.

"Come, lie down beside me," said Bellow. "It's a chilly night tonight; I'll keep you nice and warm."

All three lay there and within half an hour, were sound asleep.

Not long into the night, a dozen inquisitive gnomes came creeping along. Earlier, as the threesome passed through their town, the gnomes noticed just how pretty Tianaju was. They were fascinated, and all wanted a closer look at her. The nearer they crept, the lovelier she looked. The princess was so beautiful, the gnomes decided to kidnap her. All gnomes can be extremely quiet. So, creeping up to her, they put a hand around the startled princess's mouth, picked her up, and carried her off to a large wooden cottage. The terrified princess was tied to a chair and asked an abundance of tormenting questions.

"Who are you? Where do you come from? Where are you going? How are you so beautiful? Are you a witch? Tell us now, or we will torture you until you do."

As the night went on, the gnomes began arguing, fighting and shouting so much that more and more gnomes came to join in. Every male gnome wanted to marry the princess, and all the lady gnomes hated her.

One such spiteful lady rubbed mud in the princess's face, threw her pack in the fire, and tore at her clothes.

"She's a fairy!" Shouted the lady gnome. Look! Look at her folded wings? Tear them off."

The terrified princess, thinking she was about to die, cried out for her father. Then, suddenly there was an almighty crash and a deafening roar. It was Bellow. The massive elk had smashed through the side of the cottage and was stood there shaking his head, furiously snorting, with his eyes a blazing red.

"STAND ASIDE," he roared. "Or you will surely die tonight. Pheler, untie the princess and woe betides anyone who tries to stop you."

Pheler rushed to Tianaju who was slumped over with her head on her chest as if dead. The princess thinking she was about to suffocate, had fainted from the trauma of it all. It was the gnomes turn to be terrified now, and as they ran, scattering everywhere, Bellow chased them.

"If I ever see you again, it will be at your peril," roared the furious elk.

Pheler revived the princess, who was still upset and shaking with fear.

"Thank you, Pheler," she said feebly. "I thought I was going to die."

The elf told her what Bellow had done and how he drove away the bad jealous gnomes. They had to wait at the weeping willows until he returned, and that's where he quickly took the distressed princess.

Half an hour later, the elk arrived, his whole body steaming, and with a worried look in his eyes.

"Are you alright, Princess? Did they hurt you and take your gold?"

"Yes, I am alright, thank you, dear Bellow," replied Tianaju, feebly. "I still have my purse of gold, but they threw my pack of clothes and things into the fire."

The beautiful princess, looking down at herself, began to cry.

"Oh, I must look a terrible sight. My face and hair are so dirty, and my clothes are all torn."

Bellow, still breathing deeply, replied, "No, Princess, no. Even covered in mud and your clothes torn almost to rags. No one, and I mean no one, is more beautiful than you."

"Yes, I agree," added Pheler. "Your beautiful face and your long blonde hair are the likes of which no one has ever seen; it is impossible for you to look terrible."

Princess Tianaju, still with tears rolling down her lovely face, managed to say, "You are both very kind. But what good is being blessed like I am if I cannot be loved and married?"

Pheler whispered to Bellow, "We must quickly find the stranger Etredelmah before Tianaju loses heart and give up.

"Don't worry about a thing, Princess," said Pheler. "You'll get to the moon and find your crystal. This, we promise."

Although still a little shaken, Tianaju thanked her friends, led down and the threesome slept until dawn.

Bellow was up first and gently nudged Tianaju with his nose.

"Come, my Princess. We must make haste. Wash off whatever mud you can for now. Thredeegy is where we are heading next. It is a land of riches, where elves and fairies live in great wealth. You will be safe there your Highness."

The princess washed and tidied herself the best she could. Then, after a quick breakfast of berries, Tianaju and the elf mounted the kind elk and away they went trotting across the moors, leaving Lidapler behind them.

"Yippee!" shouted Pheler. "This is such lovely countryside; I wonder if I know anyone in Thredeegy? Perhaps there's a cousin or two of mine there."

When the missionaries arrived in Thredeegy, they found everything made of marble, gold and silver. It was fantastic. After stopping outside an Inn, the elk said as he let down his friends.

"Princess, there's a store across the street where you can buy new clothes. If you and Pheler book a room for the night, you can bathe and change into them. I'm off into the woods to eat and sleep. I'll return at the crack of dawn. Until then, take care of her, Pheler."

Bellow slowly turned, sniffed the air and headed off towards the forest.

After waving until he was out of sight, the princess and Pheler crossed the street and went into the store. Tianaju chose a velvet suit, a few shawls, a lovely sky blue dress, a warm looking waterproof sleeping pouch and a few other necessities. When she had finished, she took them all to the lady storekeeper.

"I would like to buy these clothes and goods, please," said Tianaju, politely.

She handed the lady two gold coins, which was more than enough to pay for them. The storekeeper, who was looking very pompous and with her nose in the air, scoffed.

"I am very sorry, but this is not even close enough to buy these clothes, never mind the goods. I need three more gold coins, and there won't be any change, either."

Both friends looked at one another. They were disgusted with the lady's attitude and her asking price.

"How can these be so expensive?" Thought the lovely princess.

Unfortunately, she had no choice but to pay the asking price. So, Tianaju handed the storekeeper another three gold coins and said thank you. The lady fairy huffed, bade them goodbye then laughed as the two friends were leaving.

The pair just shrugged their shoulders, crossed the street and went into the Inn.

"Could we have two rooms for the night and a bath for the lady, please?" Pheler kindly asked.

"Very well, that will be three gold coins each," replied an overweight elf eating a sandwich.

"We only want to stay one night!" exclaimed Tianaju.

"Yes," replied the innkeeper, putting down his sandwich. "But it is still three gold coins, each."

Once again, Tianaju paid the asking price, for she desperately needed a bath and a bed for the night. The princess paid the overweight elf, and the companions were shown to their rooms. Within an hour, the happy princess was soaking away in a lovely bath full of soapy bubbles. She enjoyed it so much that she stayed there, soaking until the water chilled. After drying her long blonde hair, she changed into the new expensive sky blue dress she had bought earlier, then led on her comfy bed.

Later that evening, the two met on a balcony over-looking a glorious sight. Everything was made from all the precious metals and sparkling gems, imaginable. It was a luxury they had never seen before. Hurrying along, down in the streets were town folk, all heading towards what looked to be a dancehall. The clothes they were wearing suggested there was a dance that night. The princess, remembering Bellow saying that she would be safe there, suddenly had an idea.

"It may be a good idea if we were to go to the dance, Pheler. Perhaps, someone there knows Etredelmah and where he lives. Also, someone might know how to reach the moon. What do you think?"

Pheler agreed, "Well, we will never know standing here, so yes, come on, let's go. They don't look as if they are dressed for a fairy ball, so we are okay dressed the way we are."

So, off they went making their way to the dance hall. It was about eight o'clock when they arrived, and it cost two gold coins each for admission. How lovely it was inside, like nothing you could ever imagine. There were spotlights, coloured lights, floodlights, candle lights and also very nice dance music. Tianaju and Pheler took to the floor and had more than a few dances, but, as you can probably guess, the princess was constantly being watched. Not only for her looks but also for her dancing ability. One by one, Dukes, Lords, Elves and handsome fairies, made their way over to ask her to dance. Tianaju accepted, and while dancing, she took the opportunity to ask them about Etredelmah. Unfortunately, no one had ever heard of him. Some said they thought they knew him, but wanted money first. They were only after her money; not one of them knew him at all.

With the princess being continuously asked to dance, she soon became exhausted.

"That's it, I have had enough. No one has ever heard of Etredelmah. Come on, Pheler, let's go back to the Inn. I am so tired."

Meanwhile, Pheler had enjoyed himself dancing with a lady elf he knew from his old school days. He wasn't happy to go, but said goodbye to his lady friend and escorted the princess safely back to the Inn.

"Will you be alright, Princess, if I just pop back to the dance for an hour?" Pheler asked.

"Yes, I will be fine, Pheler. You go on and enjoy yourself; I am going to bed. See you in the morning."

Tianaju was so tired she just flopped down on her bed and fell asleep.

Unknown to the two friends, they had been followed, and the follower was now knocking on the princess's room door. She woke up and thinking it was Pheler she opened the door. In the doorway, was a very handsome, well-dressed fairy with a lovely smile.

"Excuse me, my lady; my name is Rathile. I hear you are looking for Etredelmah from Nuraleth? Nuraleth is the land where I was born."

"Yes, I am. Do you know him?" She quickly replied. "If so, do you know where he lives in Nuraleth, and have you seen him lately?"

Rathile smiled, "Yes, I do know him. I know him well. I have come to tell you that he is staying with me this very night. He is staying until the morning and intends to head back to Nuraleth at sunrise."

"Oh, please, can you take me to him?" Asked the excited princess. "I am so desperate to speak to him!"

The handsome fairy smiled again and replied, "How could I say no to one as lovely as you? My carriage is outside, and I will be only too happy to take you. If we go now, we'll be there in an hour."

"Thank you," said the princess putting a lovely purple shawl around her shoulders.

The beautiful princess, forgetting all about her worries, driven on by the exciting thought of meeting Etredelmah, drove off with Rathile into the mist of the night.

After about twelve miles or so, they stopped outside a grand mansion. It was lit up so brightly that you would have thought it was daylight. Greeting them at the door and wanted to be patted was Rathile's rough-haired dog. Once inside, Tianaju could see that this was a very posh fairy's home.

"Put a light to the fire and sit down; I will tell Etredelmah you are here," said Rathile.

He went away and was gone for about half an hour. During that time, the anxious princess lit a nice little fire. When Rathile finally returned, he came back looking distressed.

"I have sad news; Etredelmah is not here. He left a note saying that he had to go."

The disappointed princess cried out in anguish, "Oh no! You told me he was staying until sunrise. What am I to do now?"

Rathile suggested she stay the night, and he would take her to Etredelmah in the morning.

Tianaju replied, "Thank you kindly, Sir, but I am with two friends of mine. If I don't return tonight, they will be worrying about me. So I had better be going now. There is no need for you to take me. I'll fly back myself."

She thanked him again, said goodbye and walked towards the door. But, as she reached it, she found herself being held by Rathile's magic.

"No, please! Please don't go! Come with me; I want to show you something," said Rathile.

Tianaju was frightened now. She had no powers of her own and didn't like being held this way. So she had to relax and be crafty.

"Very well. I'll stay," she replied. "But why are you holding me? There is no need."

Rathile released her from his magic and replied, "Oh, I'm sorry, but it's just that you are so beautiful; I thought I would never see you again. I just want to show you something, then perhaps you might change your mind and stay."

The princess now realised that Etredelmah was never there at all. It was just a trick. She knew that the only thing to do was to play along with Rathile for a while.

"Come with me," said Rathile.

They walked through a long corridor that led them to the back of the house. Rathile opened a door into a factory full of workers. They were all sewing away, making lovely clothes and shoes. Rathile then said as he held Tianaju's hand.

"I have workers here day and night. I live a comfortable life and have more than enough to buy anything I want in the world. Now come this way, I have one more thing to show you."

Rathile led her back through the corridor until they reached a room on the other side of the mansion. Inside, neatly stacked, were wooden chests that Rathile claimed to be full of gold and jewellery. In the middle of the room were two beautiful, hand-carved, solid oak thrones.

"I am a Duke, and these are my thrones," said Rathile as he sat on one. "I have them ready for when I rule over this land."

He told Tianaju that long ago, he rebelled against his father because he didn't like how he treated the people of Aslarill. So, on his twenty-first birthday, he moved out, came here and was now waiting to make Threedeegy his kingdom.

The princess was exasperated with it all and didn't know what to say. Thinking the Duke must be genuine, she found herself liking him again. Then, out of the blue, Rathile went down on his knee.

"Will you marry me and be my wife? Share my wealth and rule my kingdom with me. We will want for nothing; neither will our people."

Sitting down on a chest, the princess remembered her terrible fate and couldn't believe what she was hearing and began to cry. It was everything she had been dreaming of.

"Oh Rathile," said the sobbing princess. "I do so want to marry, have children and be queen one day. I would give anything and everything that is mine if only I could."

"Well, marry me now, and all your dreams will come true," replied the Duke. "I fell in love with you the moment I saw you at the dance. You are the most beautiful living fairy I have ever seen."

"I'm sorry, Rathile, but I cannot marry you," sobbed the princess.

"Why not?" asked Rathile, who was now looking more than anxious.

"I must first find Etredelmah, for my destiny lies with him," she replied.

The Duke was angry and raised his voice, "What does he have that I cannot give you."

"The key to my heart," she replied. "He holds the key to my heart and life."

Hearing this, Rathile flew into a rage, rushed towards the princess, shouting and waving his wand.

"So, you love him! Him! Etredelmah, do you? That's what it is?" he raged.

The terrified princess lifted up her hands to protect herself and cried out, "Please! Oh, please don't hurt me," she begged.

At that moment, Rathile stopped in horror. For as the princess raised her hands to protect herself, he saw the burn mark on the palm of her hand.

"It's you! It's you!" He roared. "You're the one. You're the one that's cursed. Everyone I know talks about you. I should have known by your beauty you were her. Why didn't you tell me? Get out of my house; you are of no use to me. Go, get out!"

Tianaju ran back down the corridor, out through the door and flew into the air, constantly looking behind her. The poor princess was in a desperate state of mind and body now, and it was taking all her strength to fly and keep going. Although thinking she would never get back to the Inn again, she arrived just before dawn. Exhausted now, she flew into her room, collapsed on the bed, but happy to be away from that nasty Duke. She knew Bellow was fetching her at dawn, but she couldn't keep her eyes open and drifted off to sleep.

The princess had only been asleep a short while when she heard Bellow calling her. He was now wondering where she was and if anything had happened to her. She rushed to the balcony and told him that she was okay and would be with him in five minutes. She felt safe now and was so happy to see him again that she just piled her clothes into her sleeping pouch, flew out over the balcony, down into the street to the waiting elk.

"Where's Pheler?" she asked.

"We have sad news, Princess," replied the solemn elk. "Pheler has met a lady elf and has fallen in love. He has decided to stay here in Threedeegy to be close to her and hope they'll marry one day. He could not bring himself to tell you personally. He apologises for letting you down and will be praying that you'll soon climb that mountain and claim your happiness."

The princess thought about her ordeal with Rathile and her heart sunk. It was like two bad, terrible nightmares that had just come true.

"Well, princess, that's life, but we must go on. Come, your highness, tie your pouch around my neck and climb upon my back. We must be on our way to hopefully be in Iwedilli by next week."

Princess Tianaju, although sad and feeling very depressed and tired from the night before, tied her pouch around the elk's neck and flew up onto his soft, warm back. Within an instant, they were away again, heading west with the sun behind them.

Four

I wedilli was a few hundred miles away, but the companions should make it there comfortably in about seven days.

While stopping in numerous forests to eat and sleep, Bellow introduced the princess to many of his friends. Bellow also managed to meet a few of his sons and daughters. They all happened to be living in the area. With such a happy family gathering, they all had great fun playing tag and hide and seek.

Tianaju was feeling much better now and had put all that happened in Thredeegy and Lidapler behind her. Once again, she was totally focused on her mission and was looking forward to arriving in Iwedilli.

After three days of travelling, the pair had reached Jackdaws Quarry and were making their way through it. It was a lovely day. The princess was enjoying the ride, thinking, and talking aloud to herself.

"One more day after Iwedilli, and we'll be in Hetraleonie. Oh, I wish it would hurry up."

"Patience, my Princess," said Bellow. "It will be far from over. The land beyond Iwedilli, until you reach Hetraleonie, is a treacherous place and will be difficult to cross."

"Oh, no! How difficult do you mean?" Asked the beautiful Tianaju.

"I tell you solemnly, Princess. You must prepare yourself for that journey, for it's an extremely cold land, the coldest in all of Fairyland. It's winter all year round, and no one lives there. It is only seven miles wide and eight miles long, but in that perishing cold wintery land, every mile will seem like ten."

Feeling very low again, she asked the mighty elk the name of the land.

"Apsinider, The land is called Apsinider," said Bellow while shaking his head.

The princess remembered what Bellow had said to her back in the woodland of Gingers.

"Only as far as Iwedilli, that's what he said," she muttered. "I'll be too frightened and never make it on my own."

Thinking this, she leaned over, put her arms around the elk's neck and sadly asked.

"Bellow, after Iwedilli, are you coming with me through Apsinider?"

The elk sighed and gave a little smile before replying, "You are my princess, and I love you. My heart and body are yours now and forever. So, yes, Princess, I will be with you all the way. I will die first before I would ever leave or let anyone hurt you."

Tianaju squeezed her arms tighter around his neck and said, "Thank you, Bellow, I love you too."

For two more days, Bellow and Princess Tianaju travelled on; each day heading west until they came alongside a river. On the other side of this river was a huge forest that looked to be going on and on. The elk stopped and said as the princess jumped down.

"On the far edge of that forest lies a thick enchanted border of trees. Beyond it is human land. This thick borderline cannot be penetrated by anyone, not even fairies. It is through this forest and to the enchanted border we must go. So now, while I swim across this river, you can fly over and wait for me on the other side."

The elk walked into the river until all you could see of him were his head and antlers. As he swam across, Tianaju hovered above, singing a little song. When over the other side, the soaking wet elk shook himself down and almost drenched the poor princess, but she just backed away and laughed.

"Let me just dry off, then we'll be on our way before it gets dark," said Bellow.

After an hour's rest and something to eat, our two companions set off through the forest, keeping to a secret path. There were lots of lovely flowers growing along the way, all enjoying the sun as it shone through the trees.

With the night almost upon them, the elk searched around and found a place to lie down. The princess slipped into her sleeping pouch and lay down beside him to keep warm. While she lay there admiring the stars twinkling through the trees, Bellow said something unexpected.

"In the enchanted border, there are two willow trees. These willows are the gateway in to the human world. Beyond them is the village of Cleremun. It is into this human village you must go. It is the only place to buy human clothing, clothing that will protect you from the cold and bitter winds of Apsinider. You need these clothes because it will be impossible for you to fly through that desperate land. The air is heavy, and the north wind is far too strong."

Tianaju trusted her faithful friend, and whatever he suggested, she knew it was in her best interest. So, with a happy, contented sigh, she carried on looking at the stars until dropping off to sleep.

After a restful night, the morning seemed to come too quickly for her. Then, as she yawned, stretched and was just about to open her eyes, she felt her face being gently washed.

"Good morning, beautiful. I see you are with the big fella," said a lovely red squirrel. "We heard you were coming, so we brought you some nuts and berries for breakfast. It's a lovely morning and time the pair of you were up."

A few more squirrels came scuttling down the trees to join him.

"Hey, how are you getting on Skittle, my old friend?" Asked the elk as he stood up to stretch.

"Oh, we are alright, can't complain, Bellow. There's plenty for us to eat this time of year, so we are just enjoying ourselves getting fat and stocking up for the winter."

Tianaju laughed, tidied up her pouch and clothes then sat down with Skittle and his friends. She thanked the squirrels for their gifts and thoroughly enjoyed them while Bellow strolled around munching nice juicy leaves.

With breakfast finished, Bellow, Skittle and his friends put together a plan. How to get the beautiful princess in and out of Cleremun without drawing too much attention to her. Something that certainly wasn't going to be easy.

Once in the village, Bellow suggested, "Do not try the clothes and boots on your Highness. Buy the next size up from your natural size, but before you go, I'll check out the route from the border into Cleremun. I need to make sure it's clear and safe for you."

Skittle warned the elk, "The hunters in Cleremun are shooting every kind of animal or any bird that moves. They sell their skins and antlers at the market there. They even sell the bird's feathers. Yes, O powerful one, if ever they happen to see you, even half a mile away, you will be in serious trouble."

Two hours of daylight had now passed. Before setting off, Bellow asked the squirrels to spread the word of their plan to all their friends and would they keep a lookout in the treetops of Cleremun. After bidding each other goodbye, Tianaju and the great elk set off across the forest to the enchanted border.

They travelled on with the sun beaming through the trees, keeping them warm. It also gave a lot of light to a beautiful forest. Bellow stopped at a nice small patch of grass and shrubs to eat and rest. The princess searched around for some fruit to go with the nuts given to her by Skittle and his friends.

"Enjoy the warmth of the sun now Princess," said Bellow. "For when you are back safely from Cleremun, we'll trek back through this forest to Iwedilli then into Apsinider. There you will be greeted by the cold north wind. He will be blowing in extremely cold weather, and for three long days, the struggle against him will be severe. Once you are through this torment, you will be in Hetraleonie with Etredelmah, this I promise."

The princess then said to herself, "Why does he keep saying, you, all the time? I thought he was coming with me? Ah, perhaps it's just the way he talks?"

Eventually, they came to a suitable resting place to sleep for the night. Apart from the occasional hoot of a tawny owl, the pair had a reasonably good night's rest and were up early, setting out once more after breakfast.

"Today, Princess, we have to carry out our plan," said the great elk as they trotted along.

"Yes, Bellow," she replied. "I know what to do."

It was midday before Bellow stopped under an old ancient ash tree and told the princess to rest. Later, he would check out the route through Cleremun to make sure the human path was safe. So, after they had their lunch and relaxed, it was time for Bellow to check out the route.

"Right Princess, I had better be off now. You'll be safe here until I return. It shouldn't take me too long. While I am away, you can prepare yourself as we planned."

As Bellow trotted off through the forest, Tianaju shouted out, "Be careful, Bellow. Remember what Skittle told you."

Bellow smiled then as he disappeared through the trees, he shouted back, "Don't worry. I will!"

The princess unpacked her pouch and took out what little clothes she had. Having only a choice of two garments, one being the sky blue dress she was already wearing, the other a dark green velvet dress and jacket with silk pockets and buttons. She rolled the green dress and jacket over and over in the dry dust. She did this because part of their plan was to make the clothes look old and inconspicuous; it was the only thing to do. After undressing and putting on her now dusty green dress and jacket, she laughed. She had never looked so shabby. With her wings now neatly tucked away underneath her dress and jacket, she took the sleeping pouch and looped it over her head and shoulders. Hopefully, this was going to make her look like a traveller. Tearing up that lovely sky blue dress was sad for her, but it made a handy scarf to cover her tied-up hair. Finally, she rubbed her hands in the dust and lightly patted her beautiful face. The princess was now ready and sat down to wait for Bellows return.

She waited patiently for an hour before she saw him coming through the trees.

"Sorry I'm late, my Princess. I had to make sure it was safe for you. As soon as you are out of the enchanted forest, some of the animals in Cleremun are not very friendly and could be hostile towards you. But after checking it all out carefully, I found it quite safe for the rest of the day. I'll walk with you to the two willows. From then on, you must go alone."

The princess said she understood and was ready. Saying that, diving out of the clear blue sky and swooping down beside them, flew a glorious buzzard. He held a soft green purse in his beak, which he placed in the princess's hand.

"Your father, the great King Drahol, sends you this and his love."

Bellow was happy to see him, "Ah, well done Sharpy," said the elk.

Bellow told the princess that he had sent Sharpy to ask the king for some dollars.

Tianaju was puzzled now and asked why because she had money.

The elk replied, "Yes, but gold coins are not used in Cleremun; everything there is paid for in dollars."

After thanking Sharpy and saying goodbye, she climbed onto the back of her amazing, faithful friend and away they went through the forest. The elk followed the path westward for a mile until pulling up in front of the very dense enchanted borderline. The border was so thick with trees of all shapes and sizes, it was impossible to see through them. Bellow stooped, to let Tianaju down in front of two enormous weeping willow trees. Each tree had thousands upon thousands of branches, and every branch was hanging down, touching the earth below.

"Be careful now, my Princess," said the caring elk. "Follow our plan and all things should go well. Do not attempt to fly, for if there are hunters around, they will surely see you. If things do go wrong, the squirrels will inform me."

"Don't worry my dear friend," replied the princess. "I intend to be careful, and I shall see you soon."

Calling from behind her now were two mellow sounding voices, "This way Princess."

It was the willow trees. They were now opening up their branches, forming a long narrow archway leading into the human world.

"Follow the human path through their forest, and you will reach Cleremun in an hour," said the willows'.

The princess kissed Bellow on the nose, said goodbye to her worried-looking friend, then slowly walked through the long dark archway into the human land of Cleremun.

"Good luck now," wished the willows' as they closed their branches' behind her.

Tianaju set off through the human forest, telling herself that she was going to be strong. She was determined to succeed for she so desperately wanted to find Etredelmah. After about a mile, she came out onto a road. There now, to the left, half a mile away, was the village of Cleremun. She sighed, took a few deep breaths, then after telling herself not to be afraid, she briskly walked on into the village, humming a tune.

Cleremun is a very well kept hunter's village and is a big tourist attraction in the winter. The streets were quite busy, and because it was, no one noticed Tianaju walking along. This made her feel a whole lot better while looking for the store she wanted. She didn't have to look too far. The outdoor shop was the largest in the village, and it was right there in the middle of the street.

"Thank goodness," she said and walked calmly through the door.

There were already customers browsing around inside. Once again, no-one said nor took any notice of her, only one person saying hello. She wandered around the store and found everything she needed, making sure the clothes and boots were one size bigger except for the socks. The princess carried them over and lay them on the counter.

"I would like to purchase these goods, please," she politely asked the lady assistant. "Could I also have that carrying bag with straps to put them in, please?"

The lady smiled and fetched the bag Tianaju had pointed to. Then, after counting the cost, said, "That will be four dollars and two cents, please."

Tianaju handed the lady five dollars and told her to keep the change. She then asked the lady if she would be kind enough to pack everything away in the bag for her. The assistant obliged and pack them neatly inside. The princess thanked her and carried her shopping outside. She then slowly undid the pouch from her back and tied it on top of the bag. With that done, she lifted the bag up onto a bench. This made it easier to slip her arms through the straps and up onto her shoulders. While she was doing all this, watching her from across the road, was a young teenage boy.

"Would you like a hand with your pack, lady?" he asked.

"No, thank you, I can manage," the princess replied.

The curious boy watched her for a while then went away. With her bag safely on her back, the princess calmly walked out of the village, back up the road and into the forest. By now, her little heart was racing with anxiety. Everything was going well. All she wanted now was to get back to the enchanted forest and Bellow.

She was a good fifteen minutes into the forest when suddenly there was a pitiful bellowing cry.

"Oh, no! That sounds like Bellow," she said aloud. "Yes, there it is again. He's in pain somewhere."

The cry was coming from the left of her into the forest. Without hesitation, she took off her pack and pushed it under a holly bush. Listening again to the continuous cries, she headed off through the forest towards it. After about five minutes of listening and searching, she finally saw a struggling animal. It was a female fallow deer, held fast in a cruel snare. When the poor deer caught sight of the princess, she struggled even more and cried out, "Oh, no! No!"

"Whoa! Steady there!" said Tianaju trying to calm the frightened female.

The startled deer immediately calmed down. She didn't seem afraid now.

"I can understand you," said the deer. "Are you a fairy? You must be."

"Yes, I am. Now keep still," replied Tianaju. "I'll set you free from the loop around your neck."

Snares pull very tight and get even tighter when an animal struggles. Eventually, the careful and caring princess managed to free what she could now see was a severely crippled deer. Once she was released, the deer was very grateful.

"Thank you," she said. "I have escaped from a cruel, fairy lord, who was banished from Fairyland. He captures every crippled animal he can find, then keeps them all either tethered up or in small pens. Tourists travel from everywhere and pay the cruel lord, in silver, just to see his deformed animals."

The deer suddenly turned to sniff the air, and as she listened, she shouted.

"Quickly, we must get away from here; it's the Lord. He's coming. Quickly now, follow me."

The deer hobbled off with the frightened princess following closely behind. Then, as the deer brushed through the trees, one of the branches sprang back, hitting the poor princess full in the stomach. The blow winded her so badly that the poor unfortunate princess fainted and collapsed.

Twenty minutes later, the princess now palpitating, groggy, and her vision partially blurred, heard someone.

"There she is, my Lord!"

On hearing this, Tianaju tried to get up but was so dizzy, she blacked out again and collapsed.

The moment Princess Tianaju regained consciousness, she found herself now in only her dress, lying on a couch, in a room with no windows. While trying to get up, she found a thick leather bracelet tied around her wrist. The bracelet was attached to a long chain, locked to an iron ring set in a large fireplace. Sitting opposite her, besides a crackling log fire, was a ginger-haired, stern-faced looking man. His dark eyes were fixed on the princess and stayed there looking for some time. Eventually, without moving, he spoke in a very meaningful, deep and hollow voice

"I am Lord Ohibronoeler, and you, my dear, are my prisoner."

Tianaju sat up, asking, "Why? What have I done?"

"Stand up!" demanded the Lord. "Come over here by the fireplace. Take a look at yourself in the mirror."

Standing up curiously, the frightened princess walked over to the mirror, and as she looked at herself, she gasped and cried out, "Oh no!"

Her face had been washed and with the back of her dress torn open, right behind her were her wings.

"That's right," roared Ohibronoeler, pushing her back over and down onto the couch.

"With a beautiful face like that and the tell-tale burn mark on the palm of your hand, you can only be one fairy. You are the daughter of the one who took away my wand and shrivelled my wings to a mere fly's. YES, you are the daughter of the one and only King Drahol of Fairyland. Well, I'll make him pay for what he did to me. Three years ago he stopped me from re-entering Fairyland, all because I flew here without permission. So you, my little princess, will marry me under the full moon, this very Sunday night. With your stunning beauty and those fantastic wings, the whole world will swarm here. Yes, my pretty one, they will pay fortunes to see my lovely fairy bride. I will be so rich and powerful, together with an army so big; I'll SMASH my way through that enchanted forest. Fairyland will be crushed, never to exist again."

He turned, gave a terrible wicked laugh, walked out and locked the door behind him.

The frightened princess stayed locked up all evening until Ohibronoeler returned at midnight with some blankets and a cape.

"You'll stay here for the night, pretty one. The room I'm preparing for you should be ready by tomorrow. Until we are married, use this cape to cover up those pretty little wings of yours. Then I'll show you, my beautiful fairy wife, to the whole wide world. I'll make your father suffer. Yes, I'll make him suffer so badly, he'll know just what misery tastes like. I tell you NOW, the beginning of the end of Fairyland has already begun. I HATE your father, and my revenge is coming his way, fast."

He then walked out slamming the door shut, locking it, once more behind him.

"Bellow, Bellow. Where are you?" cried the poor desperate princess. "Oh, my dear mother, father, please help me?"

It was no use, for out of Fairyland her pleas could not be heard. She just sobbed and sobbed until falling into a deep sleep.

In the morning, she woke to the sound of banging and shuffling around above her. On the table in front of her was a bowl of fruit. It looked horrible and didn't smell very nice, either. It had been put there while she was asleep. Within half an hour, the door opened, and the terrified princess cringed. It was Ohibronoeler again. He unlocked her chain from the fireplace, caught hold of her hair and dragged her up some stairs into a dirty room full of rubbish. The only window in there had no glass, only rusty iron bars an inch apart. The horrid lord took off her chain and pushed her across the room, causing her to fall.

"This is where you'll stay until we are married this coming Sunday," said the evil lord.

"I will never marry you. Besides, I can't marry you!" shouted the princess.

"You have no say in the matter, my dear," replied the very confident Ohibronoeler. "The Vicar works for me. Once he signs that legal document, you will be mine to do whatever I like."

Before he left the room, he looked at her with hatred now in his eyes.

"You'll be fed and treated like all my other miserable prizes. If you want to know what I'm talking about, look outside your window."

The lord, once again, walked out slamming and locking the door behind him.

Tianaju looked around and found that the room was full of cracked jugs and dishes, broken furniture, dirty smelly clothes and shoes. There were also rat droppings everywhere, and a pile of rotten stale food that the rats were probably eating. The bed was old with a bundle of sheets on top of a torn straw mattress. The princess was confused now and the thought of marrying the worst Fairy Lord that ever lived, made her heart sink so low that her throat went dry.

Climbing over the rubbish, making her way over to the window, she looked out to a very pitiful sight. There were at least a hundred animals; most of them cripples, others were unusually tall, tiny or skinny. They were on about two acres of land, and all were confined to small pens, wandering around in circles. Some were tied up on a short leash, and every animal looked weak from hunger.

"They are exactly like that horrible lord described them to be," said the distraught princess. "The poor miserable creatures. If only I had a magic wand!"

While thinking about the poor unfortunate animals and how Ohibronoeler was planning to destroy fairyland, the princess promised herself.

"I must be strong for my sake and those poor animals. I will find a way out of this terrible place, and when I am back in Fairyland, I'll tell my father about the cruel lord."

The evil lord came back once more, only to throw her a few left-over scraps that his dogs wouldn't eat.

The following day, after a terrible night's sleep, Princess Tianaju heard excited voices outside. Looking out of the window, she saw two men with rifles under their arms, talking to Ohibronoeler down in the courtyard. Also, there was the same young teenager who offered to help her at the store. She couldn't hear all that they were saying, but as the men were repeatedly pointing towards the forest, it sounded like, "They are all heading this way, my Lord!"

"What!" Shouted Ohibronoeler. "Right, men. Let's go and get them."

Away the four went galloping on their horses, with the cruel lord shouting, "The word of the day is KILL!!"

It was evening when Tianaju heard them coming back. She made her way to the window and watched them dismounting their horses. One of the men seemed to be in pain and was obviously bleeding because his shirt was red with blood. The frightened princess kept very quiet and listened, but their voices were muffled by the wind blowing through the bars of the window. She couldn't make out anything until she heard Ohibronoeler shouting out in anger, "SHE'S MINE!"

Soon after hearing those words, her heart began to race uncontrollably, for she could hear the wicked lord coming up the stairs. He unlocked the door and stood there scowling, wrinkling up his cruel green eyes. He had a bright orange dress in his hand which he flung across the room saying, in a deep, harsh voice.

"Get yourself ready by the morning, pretty one. Our wedding has been rearranged for tomorrow. Yes, my lovely avenger, you'll be mine by noon. Once we are bonded in marriage, no one, not even your father can help you. He will never ever see you again. NEVER, unless he returns my wand and gives me back my wings."

Turning, swishing his cloak behind him, the hateful Lord Ohibronoeler walked out and locked the door.

Tianaju was panicking now until she remembered the pledge she made the day before.

"I must be strong. Come on, calm down. I'll think of something. There must be a way out of here," she sighed.

Desperate now, Tianaju led on the bed, trying to think of a plan to escape. It was hopeless, and after tossing and turning for at least an hour, she was so exhausted, curled up in a ball and fell asleep.

It was two o'clock in the morning when suddenly she was awakened by a loud scream. Within minutes, Ohibronoeler came into her room, put on her chain, and dragged the screaming princess down the stairs by her hair. The horrid lord then pushed her into a large chamber. With her head paining from being dragged by her lovely hair, the princess tried to calm herself. In front of her, lying unconscious and face down on a table in the middle of the room, was the wounded man she had seen earlier.

"Clean up his wound with the hot water and cloth on the table. Then, with that needle and thread, sew him up. Make sure you do it properly, too," ordered Ohibronoeler.

This was a horrible thing to ask of her. She had never seen anything like it in her life. The princess knew that being brave and playing safe was the only answer to escape this dreadful fairy lord. So, with her head paining from being dragged around, the lovely princess did what the horrid lord demanded. When all sewn up and finished, Ohibronoeler dragged her back to her room, took off the chain, and before leaving her crying on the bed, told her to be ready by ten o'clock that morning.

By now, too tired to think anymore, Tianaju turned over on her miserable bed, gave a long sad sigh and fell asleep.

Later, after the wounded man had regained consciousness, he insisted on seeing a doctor. Obliging his friend, the banished lord helped him into his carriage and set off with the boy and the other man to the village. While all this was happening, the princess stayed sound asleep, dreaming. In her dreams, she heard a familiar voice saying, good morning, beautiful. She smiled and gave a little laugh.

"Hey, I said good morning, beautiful!" Said the familiar voice once more.

Tianaju opened her eyes and jumped straight off the bed. There, sitting on the windowsill, was Skittle, the lovely little red squirrel.

"I see you are with the bad fella this time, Princess," said Skittle. "I think I'd rather be with the big fella, wouldn't you?"

"Oh, yes, yes I would," answered the desperate princess, holding onto the bars of the window.

"Well, what are you waiting for? Open the door and let's get out of here," said the squirrel pointing to the door.

"I can't! I can't, Skittle! Ohibronoeler has locked it!" She said in anguish.

"Try using the key," said the smiling squirrel. "It's on the floor under the door. Hurry now before the bad fella gets back. He's in the village at the moment."

The excited princess rushed across the room, picked up the key and opened the door. She undid and threw down her cape, stretched out her wings, flew over the bannister, down into the hallway, through an open window, and out of that terrible house. As she stood there looking around for Skittle, she saw, standing up on a hill, with the rising sun behind him, was her powerful friend Bellow.

"Wait for me," said Skittle jumping up onto her shoulder.

"What about those poor animals?" Asked Tianaju.

"They are all gone," replied Skittle. "Bellow smashed through their pens, and we squirrels chewed their tethers. So, come on, let's get out of here. Bellow's waiting for you."

The princess flew off with skittle and was soon at Bellow's side.

"Princess, it's good to see you again. Now we must hurry away from this land. Last night my sons and I were ambushed by Ohibronoeler and other hunters. Once the banished one knows you and all his prize animals are gone, he will be furious. Now, onto my back, quickly Princess, for I know the best way out."

With a steady, cautious pace, the elk headed off, making his way towards the forest. The trio with the village behind them headed east towards the sun. The great elk made good headway through the woods and was soon greeted by the squirrels waiting at the holly tree where Tianaju had left her pack.

"Thank you," said the princess after jumping down.

"Hold on," shouted Skittle. "Let's get that bracelet off of you."

He nibbled and nibbled away until it fell to the ground. Tianaju then opened up her bag, but before putting on a jacket over her torn dress, she neatly tucked away her wings underneath it. With that done, she lifted the bag up onto a tree stump and slipped it onto her back.

"Hold on again, Princess," said Skittle, "Take these few nuts with you, and good luck."

Bellow knelt down on all fours, and after his princess climbed onto his back, away they went.

"See you later, beautiful," shouted Skittle.

"Not far to go now, Princess, and then we'll be safe," said Bellow.

A moment after uttering those words, Bellow stopped, sniffed the air, and listened.

"It's the hounds, Princess! Ohibronoeler has found you gone. He knows this route, and he's tracking us. Keep your head down now, for we must get off this path. I know another way to the willow trees."

The elk turned to his right and began weaving his way through the trees with his beloved princess hanging on for dear life. Bellow knew he could outwit Ohibronoeler, for the lord was no match for the elk in these woods. The elk's main concern was the menacing deerhounds that would soon be on his trail. Tianaju was worried, but Bellow encouraged her, saying that it was okay and not to worry. He was going to travel up a brook that would lead them to alongside the enchanted border. From then on, it was only a hundred-yard dash to the willow gates.

The elk found the brook and was now feeling a lot easier. It would help slow down the hounds. As you can imagine, travelling up this brook was not an easy task for an elk because his large antlers were nearly three feet tall and almost as wide. As they slowly weaved their way up through brook and forest, it seemed to last forever; then just when Tianaju thought they would never get out, the way ahead cleared in front of them. Once they were out into the clearing, they found themselves on the original path, about a hundred yards away from the willow trees. The princess gave a sigh of relief. They were safe now, but suddenly, the great elk stopped and sniffed the air.

"Down! Down Princess! Run for your life!" He shouted alarmingly. "Head for the willows. They'll let you in. Hurry now."

Tianaju had such a fright that she didn't know which way to run.

"That way, Quick! Quickly!" Said the elk, nodded his head towards the willows.

Bellow turned just in time to see, coming out from the forest, were two hounds that were on his trail. Standing his ground, raging with contempt towards his pursuers, he charged the first hound square in the chest, knocking him sidewards into the brush. By this time, the second hound was leaping towards him. Bellow lowered his head and caught him in mid-air, and tossed the menace crashing to the ground behind him. Bellow's nostrils were wide open now, snorting out blasts of fury. His eyes were blazing red, and the muscles of his neck and shoulders were standing out. This massive elk looked an awesome sight as he paced up and down, waiting for the next one. Then, out of the brushwood came a third hound that leapt and landed on Bellow's shoulders. Bellow spun around, and as he threw back his head, the roaring elk hooked the savage assailant and sent him yelping into a tree. The three hounds attacked twice more but suffered the same fate. They were wounded now and afraid of this massive elk and backed away, limping into the forest.

As they disappeared, Bellow heard Tianaju screaming out his name. The princess was standing by the willow trees waving and shouting.

"Bellow! Bellow! Look out! He's behind you. Hurry! Come on!"

Turning around, Bellow saw Ohibronoeler on his horse riding towards him. The elk stood his ground once more and gave out an almighty roar, terrifying the lord's horse, making it stop and turn sharply. As a result, the evil lord slid out of his saddle and fell to the ground. Quickly, Bellow put his head down and charged the wicked lord, who had since picked up his rifle and was pointing it towards the elk. BANG, a shot rang out with the bullet just missing the elk by inches. By this time, Bellow was on top of the crazed lord and caught him a glancing blow, knocking him into a small tree.

"Come on! Come on, Bellow! Hurry!" shouted the anxious princess.

The elk left Ohibronoeler sprawled out on the ground and galloped off towards the princess and the willow trees. The willows were opening up their branches to let their friends back through when, BANG, BANG, two shots rang out. Bellow veered to the right and began to zig-zag his way to avoid the bullets. Then, BANG, another shot rang out, and the great lovable elk faltered and came crashing to the ground in front of Tianaju.

"Bellow, Oh no, Bellow get up!" cried the devastated princess, just as Ohibronoeler was beginning reloading his rifle.

The great elk staggered to his feet, saying, "I'm alright, Princess. I'm alright. Now hurry, we must go."

They quickly ran through the open archway with the willows closing their branches behind them.

The cruel lord was raging now with anger. "I'll get you one day and your father. The next time you won't be so lucky!"

Safe now, back in their homeland, the desperate princess flung down her bag and rushed over to her saviour.

"Are you alright, Bellow? Oh, please tell me you are, and not wounded."

"I'm fine, your Highness. Just a little nick on the side; that's all. I lost my footing back there, causing me to stumble. Pick up your pack, for we must be heading on."

Tianaju was not at all happy with the wound on his side, but the mighty elk insisted she put her pack on and climb onto his back. She had no choice, for it was too difficult for her to fly through the forest. She could fly over it, but she didn't know her way to Iwedilli nor Apsinider. So, after saying thank you to the willow trees, the two missionaries set on their way, heading north.

Five

A couple of miles into the forest, Bellow stopped to rest by the old ash tree, while Tianaju searched around for refreshments. Bellow wasn't hungry and let Tianaju finish her berries before suggesting to carry on until nightfall.

Tianaju was worried about Bellow and his condition. Ever since the willow trees, he had been staggering quite a lot and he was bleeding. She asked him once more if he was alright. He said that once they reach the edge of the forest, he would call into his old friend the wizard. He had fixed him up many times. Knowing this, Tianaju felt that they had to hurry, but she still wasn't happy about riding her saviour. Nevertheless, despite his injury, Bellow insisted the princess rode upon his back. So, Tianaju, although reluctant to do so, did what the elk asked, but after only a few miles, the compassionate princess insisted on walking the rest of the way.

During the next few hours, the elk staggered numerous times and was weakening fast.

"Not far now, Princess," said the tired elk, stopping by a beautiful holly tree with sweet-scented honeysuckle running all over it.

"This is Iwedilli, and this is my favourite tree. It's called Mascoedeth. I have always slept here when in this part of the woods. I love the scent of honeysuckle," he said, sniffing the lovely flowers.

Bellow let Tianaju down then slumped to the ground beside the tree. Tianaju, as she looked at Bellow, was horrified to see that her saviour's chest was now red with blood.

"Oh, Bellow! Quick, where does the wizard live? Tell me? I'll bring him to you." she said, trying to stop the bleeding with her jacket.

"There is no wizard, Princess," said Bellow solemnly. "I am dying. Ohibronoeler's bullet is buried deep inside my chest. No-one can save me now, not even your father. Listen to me, Princess, there is only one road through Apsinider, and it has been there since time began. It twists and turns through rocks and trees, and the bitter north wind will be tearing into your face. Your journey's end will be only four miles away, but as I told you, each mile will seem endless.

The princess, with tears streaming down her beautiful face, was desperately insisting, "Please let me fetch someone for you? Please, Bellow, I beg you?"

"No, Princess," he replied. "Stay here and keep me company. I am getting cold now and my life seems to be nearing its end. So would you do me a great favour?"

"Yes, anything. Anything Bellow," she replied. "I will do anything for you. What is it?"

Looking up at the lovely holly tree, he replied, "Could you please bury me by this, my favourite tree? It will make me so happy to think that I will always be here."

"Oh, Bellow! Bellow! Please don't die, my dear friend. Please don't die?" cried the sobbing princess.

The elk looked into her beautiful eyes and gently nudged her with his soft nose.

"Now, I must call my sons. They will know by my call what's wrong and will come to help you bury me."

He then lifted himself up onto his haunches, put his head in the air and sounded his final call. His call was so beautiful, but, at the same time, it was the most sorrowful sound that anyone could ever hear.

Tianaju was distraught now and caressed the dying elk's head as he slowly slumped back down, struggling to speak.

"I want you to be strong now, Princess. Do not weep for me. You have a mission to accomplish. Promise me that you will finish it."

She answered him with tears still streaming down her beautiful but sorrowful face.

"I will. I promise you, I will. But Bellow, oh, Bellow, I love you so much, please don't die."

The great lovably elk then looked into her tearful eyes and whispered.

"Do you remember I promised you a while ago that I would be with you until your journey's end?"

"Yes, my dear friend. I do remember what you promised," she replied sadly.

The dying elk then managed to lift himself up onto his haunches and said, "If ever I make a promise, I always keep it. Though I may lie here forever, my spirit will always be with you."

Then, as Bellow slowly slumped back down to the ground, with his last breath, he sighed, "I love you, Princess," and died.

"NO! NO!" cried Tianaju as she hugged him sorrowfully. "Bellow, Bellow, please don't die. Oh, please don't die. I love you so much."

The heartbroken princess knelt there sobbing, caressing his lovely head; gently stroking him until his sons arrived.

Fifteen minutes after hearing their father's call, Bellow's handsome sons arrived along with two of his daughters.

"Ah, dear Father. Dear Father," said one of his daughters sadly.

Tianaju told them that their father's last wish was to be buried beside the tree where he lay.

"Yes, our father, for as long as I can remember, loved this little place," said the other daughter.

So, Bellow's wish was carried out to perfection. The grieving family and Princess Tianaju scraped away the earth from in front of the holly tree, deep enough for the faithful elk's final resting place. After the burial, Bellows eldest son, who was also six feet tall but pure white, even his antlers, walked over to the princess.

"My name is Nabalion," he said in a deep voice. "My Father informed me on the night before you were rescued in Cleremun, that if he died before Hetraleonie, it would be I that will take you through Apsinider."

"No! No! No!" Cried Tianaju, interrupting him, shaking her head. "There's been enough misery because of me. I made a pledge with your father that I would reach the moon and climb that cursed mountain. He had great faith, and so shall I. I will face Apsinider unescorted, for I now know that I have to do this alone. Thank you for offering, but the misery is mine, mine alone."

"We understand," said Nabalion. "But we will stay here with you tonight, Princess. So rest now and sleep well, because from tomorrow on, you will have very little."

All through that night, the family of elks guarded their lovely princess and kept her warm. In the morning long after the sun had risen, Nabalion woke her.

"Have your breakfast, brave one," he said as Tianaju stretched.

Patrick Madden

She had plenty of berries, but the nuts Skittle had given her were almost gone. So, after washing her hands and face in the dew of the wet grass, she sat down and enjoyed some of them. When finished, she dressed in the Arctic suit of clothes that she had bought in Cleremun then walked over to the pure white elk.

"Right," said Nabalion as he knelt down on his knees. "Quickly, climb onto my back before you get too warm in those clothes. I will take you out of this forest and into Apsinider."

Before climbing on, she picked up a stick, wrote something on Bellow's grave, tapped his grave three times then mounted his son's back. The elks circled one by one, saluting their brave father with a nod as they passed. With tears in her eyes, the princess smiled as she rode past reading aloud the message she had written, "Love you, Bellow," and waved as they trotted away.

When reaching the edge of the forest, the elks stopped, and Nabalion let the princess down. She could already feel the cold wind ahead of her and was thankful for the clothes Bellow suggested.

"Take care now, our Princess," said the eldest daughter. "Remember, you cannot get lost, there is only one route through Apsinider, and it's the one you are taking. So, goodbye now, Princess. We are all wishing you return, full of joy and happiness."

"Goodbye, and thank you," said Tianaju and walked out of the forest, into the cold north wind of Apsinider.

With her head down keeping to the only route, Princess Tianaju made slow headway for about a mile then stopped for a rest. It was a bitterly cold wind, so she found shelter behind some rocks and sat down.

After about an hour's rest, Tianaju set out once more against a wind that was getting colder and stronger every five minutes. It was not long before the bitter forceful wind made every step more and more difficult to complete. With it being so difficult now to walk, the princess had to rest every half an hour by sheltering behind large trees and rocks. This depressed the poor princess, making her feel she wasn't getting anywhere, only to the next tree. With it being winter there all year round, the trees were completely bare, with not a single leaf on any of their long, skinny branches. Even in her heavy winter clothes and pack, the princess only weighed about three and a half stone. So to make any headway at all, she had to weave her way through the trees, keeping as close to them as possible. She bravely carried on until at five o'clock, less than two miles into Apsinider, Tianaju was exhausted. She couldn't go on any more and settled down for the rest of the day in a small cave among the rocks under the shelter of trees. Tianaju, unpacked her knapsack, slipped into her sleeping pouch and thought about having some berries. Unfortunately, after taking out the handkerchief they were wrapped in, she found that most of them had been squashed. So after finishing what was left of them, she nestled down to keep warm, feeling very lonely and afraid. While lying there thinking, she remembered noticing other travellers in the distance. All with their heads down, wandering around alone, looking very miserable.

"I thought Bellow said that no one lives here," muttered the princess. "Oh, Bellow, I'm frightened now. I wish you were here with me."

Yes, and rightly so, for the beautiful princess was in a land she definitely didn't like. Even the very name Apsinider made her shudder.

During the night, the north wind drove through the trees with furious bursts. They were so vicious that at about ten o'clock, a loud crack, made Tianaju cover her head in fear. Crashing to the ground came a large bough of a tree, partially blocking the cave entrance. Thinking she was trapped, it frightened her for a while until she heard a voice, "Well, I suppose that's one way of getting down."

She sat up and listened, "Hey, beautiful. How's it going in there? Any room for an old squirrel?"

"Yes," cried the princess excitedly. "Yes, come on in Skittle; I am so happy you are here."

In popped her little charmer, Skittle, the squirrel.

"I knew it was you, Skittle. What are you doing here?" Tianaju asked.

"Oh, I just thought I'd keep an eye on you for a while," he said as he sat down. "I also have something to tell you. Etredelmah knows you are coming and is waiting for you. The pathway to the moon and mountain is where he lives. He will leave a bright light on to guide you. So, be strong now, Princess, for it's only a few more miles to peace and happiness."

The beautiful princess was pleased with the good news and thanked him. She then settled down into her sleeping pouch again with the cheeky little squirrel cuddling up to her until they fell sound asleep.

After a stormy night, Tianaju woke to find that she was alone again.

"Oh, no! Where's Skittle? Skittle, where are you?" she cried, crawling outside looking for him.

"I'm up here, Princess, looking for something for us to eat. I'll be down in a minute," replied the little squirrel.

"Watch you don't fall and hurt yourself," shouted the princess.

Skittle just laughed, jumped to another branch and said, "Yeah, that'll be the day."

He took quite a few trips up and down the trees, rummaged around many rocks, but came back sadly shaking his head.

"Ah, it's hopeless Princess. There isn't a single nut or a berry to be found, not even a shell."

She stroked his head and gratefully said, "It's alright Skittle. Don't worry; I'm okay. What are your plans now? Are you coming with me?"

"No, Princess. I will have to leave you now. We squirrels are only allowed once in a lifetime in Apsinider. I have been here a day already and believe me, Princess; one day is more than enough for anyone."

That wasn't a very encouraging thing to say to the princess, but she cheerfully responded.

"Very well, Skittle. I had better be on my way. The sooner I get to Hetraleonie and Etredelmah, the better."

She then lifted her pack up onto her shoulders and turned to her friend.

"Goodbye, dear Skittle. See you when I come back," she said and with her head down, walked on.

"Yeah, see you later, beautiful. Have faith now, Princess; you can do it!" shouted the squirrel as he watched her struggling to weave her way through the trees.

So, still with her head down and leaning forward, Tianaju slowly battled her way against the force of a bitterly cold north wind.

It was two o'clock in the afternoon before she decided to stop behind some fallen trees. Cold and with her tummy rumbling from nothing to eat, she slipped into her sleeping pouch. Her moral was down now, lower than she had ever felt in her life. It was not only because she was suffering, she felt so guilty. It was because of her, Bellow had lost his life.

"But why? Why did he have to die because of me? He was so kind and lovely. It is I that should have died, not him. I have no life, he had everything to live for. Oh, what have I done? I hate myself now. Oh, Bellow, please forgive me."

With all this going on in her mind, the princess felt she didn't want to go on anymore, but if she didn't, then Bellow would have died for nothing. So, eventually, after packing away her pouch, the demoralised princess, set out once more, only this time half-heartedly. Another reason for this change of heart was, instead of trees there was now rough open land, stretching about a mile. Even so, she trekked on and with her mind constantly wandering, she cried out.

"Why! Why did this happen to me? And why do I have to suffer, so? Why can't I be loved and get married? It's so unfair. I love everyone, even the animals."

"LOOK OUT!" shouted someone, with a familiar deep sounding voice.

Tianaju had veered off the trail and was six feet away from a treacherous bog. The voice startled her, and as she straightened up, she stumbled and lost her balance. Instantaneously the fierce north wind blew the lightweight princess back against the bank. Her knapsack cushioned her fall, but she badly jarred her elbow and shoulder. She lay there in agony for about ten minutes, crying in pain until it eased. She then slowly sat up and looked around.

"Who was it that warned me?" she asked herself, hoping to see someone.

There was no one to be seen, not even an animal. The princess's arm was too painful now to carry the knapsack anymore, so she took out her sleeping pouch, slipped it around her neck and struggled back up onto the trail again. Looking ahead, she saw that there were trees now in the distance. They were only about five hundred yards away, but as the injured princess made her way towards them, every step seemed forever.

Eventually, she reached the shelter of the woods and searched around for somewhere to rest. It wasn't until late in the evening that she finally found an ancient chestnut tree with a large hole in the trunk. This was an ideal place to sleep out of the wind and cold. Exhausted now, thirsty and hungry, the princess climbed inside the hole, slipped into her pouch and fell asleep.

Poor little Tianaju was now so tired that as she slept, she dreamt a million dreams with her mind wandering everywhere and nowhere all at the same time. She was only less than a mile away from Etredelmah. So near, but unfortunately, the brave princess had reached the very limit of her endurance. Sadly, unknown to her, she was rapidly dehydrating. Hardly breathing, she lay asleep dreaming for hours until she woke feeling the pain from her injured arm. It had swollen while she slept. While lifting herself up into a better position, she heard a whistle. The exhausted princess was so weak she could barely open her eyes to see who it was that whistled. Peeping out from under her hood, she saw a bright light in the distance.

"Have I made it? Am I here?" She muttered. "Oh, but I'm so tired, I don't know if I want to see him anymore, now. What's the point? I can never be happy knowing that Bellow lost his life because of me. This whole task was just a waste of time and life. I'm so selfish."

Disheartened, she closed her eyes and drifted off far away, thinking about her family and friends she had left behind. While the unhappy princess dreamt about the past, a whistle sounded again. Slowly, she opened her tired eyes. The light she had seen earlier was a lot closer now. With her eyes being so heavy, she couldn't keep them open long enough to focus, but she didn't care. She just slipped back to sleep, moving only to adjust her painful shoulder. The badly demoralised and dehydrated princess, thinking she would never see her family and friends again, accepted the fact that she was going to die. Then suddenly, as she cried out from jarring her shoulder, she heard the sound of music and singing. It was a sound like nothing she had ever heard. It was so beautiful that she opened her weary eyes and saw that the gleaming light was now close by. The light, although bright, was soft and warm not at all dazzling. It was so soothing and was coming from what looked to be a gate about two hundred yards away. So, Tianaju made an effort, struggled out from the tree and slowly crawled towards the wonderful sight.

Spirited on by the lovely music and singing, she managed to reach the glorious gate. All the precious metal and beautiful jewels she had ever seen could never equal the beauty and elegance of such a gate. She knelt there, and while holding on to this beautiful creation, she was looking into another spectacular sight. Once again there were breath-taking trees and flowers in colours she had never seen. The sweet music she could hear came from birds, and the singing was in the air above her. Leading from the gateway up through the trees was a long wide path, bordered by the prettiest of flowers.

The princess's eyes were so blurred, she could only just make out a figure walking down the path towards her. It was a beautiful young lady who came up to Tianaju, smiled and asked if she could do anything for her.

"Yes. I'm looking for a young man by the name of Etredelmah. He lives somewhere near Hetraleonie. Do you know him?" Asked the feeble princess, in not more than a whisper.

"Yes, I know Etredelmah, but he is away on a mission, cleaning up Nuraleth."

"Oh, no! No!" cried the princess, collapsing to the ground.

"Why are you looking for him?" asked the lady.

Princess Tianaju was so despondent now; she just didn't care.

"Oh, it doesn't matter anymore," she replied sadly. "I have been wasting my time all along. I have been such a fool, but could you please, at least tell me who you are and the name of your beautiful place?"

"My name is Tanyadurew, and this is Esarapid," replied the lady.

Tianaju, although pale, drawn and severely ill, still managed to ask politely.

"Could you please let me in? I am so tired and don't want to die out here in the cold."

Tanyadurew, now sympathetic towards the princess smiled, and with a soft, kind voice, replied.

"Certainly, and you are more than welcome, but, before I do, can you tell me your name?"

"My name is Tianaju. Princess Tianaju and I come from Vanbolena."

"Now, pray tell me Princess Tianaju. What is the meaning of your name?" asked the lady.

"I don't know. I don't know," cried the princess with tears streaming down her pale, beautiful face.

Tanyadurew looked at her sadly, and with tears also in her eyes, said to the princess.

"I'm sorry, so sorry, Princess Tianaju. But no one can enter Esarapid without knowing the meaning to their name."

The sobbing princess clung to the gates and pleaded with the lady.

"Oh, please! Please! I will give you all the gold I have if I could only come into your lovely place. I just want to die happy."

With a look of sadness, the lady slowly shook her head sympathetically before replying.

"Once again, Princess. I am so very sorry. Even though you are the most beautiful fairy I have ever seen, without a meaning to your name, you cannot enter this gate."

After saying this, Tanyadurew turned and slowly walked away.

The princess now sobbing uncontrollably, managed to crawl her way back to the tree for shelter. She was so tired and cold now, and with her injured arm, it was too difficult for her to get back into her pouch. So she just wrapped it around herself and gently led down, her face streaming wet with tears.

"Why did he do this to me? Why am I being punished? Oh, Bellow, I wish I had never taken a bite of that apple. I'm sorry, so very sorry. Please forgive me?"

With her face now frozen from the tears she was shedding, and with her grieving heart heavy with sorrow, the princess no longer wanted to live. Closing her eyes, hoping she'd never wake up, she heard a voice calling out her name.

"Princess. Princess Tianaju, can you hear me? I have a message for you. It's from a very important person."

She could hear the voice clearly but was unable to respond. She had given up. Her will to live had diminished, and our brave unfortunate princess was dying. There was nothing anyone could do for her now, but, still, the kind voice continued calling.

"Princess. No one can fly to the moon. The task you set out to achieve has been accomplished. You have climbed your mountain, and your reward shall be great. The message I have is; open your eyes Princess Tianaju for the River of Diamond Crystals is waiting for you."

Listening to what the voice was saying, the princess felt a strange sensation in her heart as if someone was cuddling it. Suddenly, our lovely princess began to feel warm and happy and could now sit up and look around. Her swollen arm was healthy again, and the unbearable pain had gone. Night had fallen, and the pure white moon shone brightly above her. To her amazement, the beautiful gate and Esarapid had vanished. Even the cold north wind was no more. Then much to her delight, her heart skipped and she sighed. Opposite the princess now, sitting under a chestnut tree, in a beam of light, eating an apple, was Etredelmah.

"Well, I see you made it then, Princess Tianaju. What took you so long?" joked Etredelmah. "But now, you had better hurry, because whatever you do, don't miss this one," he said, pointing to the full moon.

"Oh, Etredelmah! I have travelled miles to see you! How can I get my little Trish back?" asked the princess.

He smiled at her and said, "Well, if you don't hurry out of those heavy clothes and dress for flying, you will never find out. So quickly now, beside the tree is your bag. Inside is a newly prepared yellow dress, made just for you."

The princess being so excited and warm now, discarded her heavy winter clothes and quickly slipped into her lovely new yellow dress with Welsh gold braided edges and buttons.

"You look so beautiful now, Princess," remarked Etredelmah. "In fact, my favourite colour is yellow, and I look pretty good on it too."

While pointing to the curved branches in the chestnut tree, Etredelmah said, "You have five minutes before the beams of the full moon reach the centre of this specially prepared archway. From then on, the moon will be held still by the one who sent me."

Etredelmah then smiled, and before walking slowly away, he bid his farewell.

"My beautiful Princess, it has been an honour, but now we must part our ways. Perhaps we will meet again one day, but until then, I'll never be too far away. So, be happy now, Princess Tianaju, you have earned it."

He gentle bowed opened up his beautiful wings and quietly flew away.

The princess didn't know what to say, for it all happened so fast. One minute Etredelmah was there, the next he was gone. She had no time to think and was all ready to go when she put her hands to her face in disbelief.

"Oh, no!" she cried. "Please, no! Where is my crystal? He didn't tell me where it is. Where's he gone now? Oh why! Why has he done this to me again? I wish...."

Suddenly, she felt her heart being cuddled again and clasped it. Immediately, her anguish left her, and she smiled. There, on the breast of her dress, was a brooch.

"It's a Guardian Angel, and he has my little Trish in his hand. Oh, thank you," she said, gazing up at the sky.

With the moon now beaming through the centre of the arch, the delighted princess flew away in anticipation, enjoying herself flying through the lovely warm beams of the moon.

Soon, the River of Diamond Crystals was in view, and as she arrived at this wonderful place, the tiny skylark was there to greet her.

"Hello, Princess Tianaju, I have been expecting you for some time now," said the pretty little skylark.

"Hello Calandra, you remember me then?" Tianaju asked.

"Oh yes, I remember you alright, Princess Tianaju. How could I ever forget one as beautiful as you? Go now, pass through and into the Royal River of Diamond Crystals to complete your long-awaited ceremony. Fly to the sacred font and place your crystal into its consecrated water."

"Thank you, Calandra," she said and gave him a lovely smile.

The happy skylark soared into the air, singing as he went. Then, with a wave of his wing, he opened up the dazzling diamond and emerald gates, letting the beautiful princess pass through. As she entered the lovely river of floating purple diamond crystals, she carefully took her little Trish out from the Guardian Angel's hand. Then, while holding it firmly, she flew through the soft crystals up to the magnificent sparkling font and hovered there. She was very nervous now, so after taking a few deep breaths, she carefully placed the crystal into the font's ice-cold water.

Immediately, a pure white dove rose out of the font and stayed hovering above Tianaju's head. The lovely dove made her feel so wonderful that little tears began to form in her eyes. Then as one of her tears fell, it burst into a shower of raindrops, every drop a different colour. Instead of falling, the raindrops continually circled the princess, covering her in a dome of colour. Tianaju, now full of joy, shouted out.

"Yes! At last. At last! It's Juanita. The meaning of my name is Juanita, the Grace of God. And the meaning of the emerald is to be Christened."

Excited now, she heard a small rumble of thunder, and a firm kind voice spoke to her.

"Tianaju. Dear Princess Tianaju. I am the Father of all creation. It was I that borrowed your crystal, causing you hardship and sorrow. It was I who set you all the different tasks, bringing you misery and pain. You were born exceptionally beautiful for this purposeful lesson alone. My wish for you, is that when the sun goes down, and bedtime approaches, you must prepare yourself to travel the world and tell every child your once in a lifetime story. They must rid themselves of the black shadow they were born with, for no one, no one with it, can enter my glorious Kingdom. Also, perpetrators of wicked evil acts, unless they repent and genuinely change their ways, will suffer the miserable pain of being lost forever.

Now, Princess Tianaju, for all your pain and sufferings, you will be rewarded with great honours. On the night of the next full moon, you shall be crowned and known as 'The Emerald Queen of Children.' You are the most beautiful fairy there will ever be, and you will live forever. So, go. Go now and be happy, Princess Tianaju."

The princess suddenly felt a warm feeling in the palm of her hand and when she looked, found that the nasty burn mark was no more. It had disappeared, but now, on her index finger was a solitary green emerald nestled in a band of Welsh gold. The dome of coloured raindrops slowly faded away along with the dove disappearing into the font.

"Oh thank you, thank you, thank you!" shouted the happy princess as she flew off, heading home to Vanbolena.

The moonbeams led her to the edge of the enchanted forest where she landed beside the wide river. She was delighted to be back and happily walked along the river bank. Then just when she was about to fly off again, a voice called out.

"Hey, beautiful. How're things. I see you made it then."

"Oh, Skittle. Where are you? I am so happy now," replied the excited princess.

Skittle was up a tree and was also excited and shouted down to Tianaju, "I'm up here, Princess. I'll be down now. You can tell me everything then."

Tianaju sat with the squirrel and told him everything that had happened to her. After listening to his beloved princess, Skittle said that he knew she was safe thirty minutes ago.

"How did you know? Who told you?" asked the curious princess.

"Look! Look, Princess. There is no shadow on the moon now. It's gone."

"Well! So it is," said Tianaju in surprise. "It must have represented the black mark I was born with. You must come to Vanbolena with me, Skittle. Help me share the good news with my family and Fairyland. I could never have completed my mission if it wasn't for you and dear Bellow.

"I will, but on one condition. I get a kiss from the most beautiful fairy in the entire world," said the cheeky Skittle.

"Come here, you lovely little squirrel, you," said Tianaju and kissed his pretty little nose.

"Wee-hee, yippee dippee," squealed the excited squirrel as he did a few skips and a somersault.

"Oh, you beauty you, I will remember that for as long as I live. Come on, let's go to Vanbolena," said the happy squirrel.

"Hop up onto my back, and we'll be on our way," said the princess who was now aching with laughter.

Away they went, heading east, homeward to Vanbolena singing a little rhyme as they went.

'The moon's so bright; no shadow is shown.

Oh, hear my delight; my meaning is known.'

After hours of flying, they flew down to rest in the forest outside Lidapler, but far enough away from those naughty gnomes of the village. The sun had risen, but Tianaju was tired and decided to stay and rest all day until the following morning. Skittle went off to collect a few nuts while Tianaju searched for berries. As night drew in, they gathered up a pile of leaves, lay down and slept until they woke as the sun rose high in the east.

Six

The two friends flew off once more, arriving in Vanbolena at about one o'clock. King Drahol and Queen Roaniler were so happy to see their daughter that they hugged and hugged her. They then listened to their princess as she told them all about her ordeal she had to endure and that the Father of all Creation, wants her to inform every child throughout the world, the importance of being Christened. The king thought it was an exceptional honour and was delighted.

"So, my dear daughter, at last, you know the meaning of your name. Pray tell me. What is it?"

She joyfully answered, "Yes, I have, dear Father. It's the Grace of God."

The king praised his beloved daughter and announced the good news throughout the whole of Fairyland.

After four weeks of preparation, it was now the night of the full moon. Fairies from all over Fairyland had gathered, waiting for the most important procession and ceremony they were ever going to witness. Princess Tianaju was on her way to be crowned and honoured with great privileges. It was a special night. Even the bight full moon and the uncountable twinkling stars shone like never before. As the Princess passed through the brightly lit streets in her magnificent carriage, everyone cheered and waved their flags. Our beautiful princess wore a stunning yellow silk dress with Welsh gold braiding and matching shoes. The gold braiding, was once again, spun by the only gold spinning spider in the world. Just above her heart, pinned to her amazing dress, was a golden Guardian Angel holding a little emerald crystal in his hand. Her fabulous robe was a stunning colour purple, interwoven with gleaming emeralds and dazzling diamonds that glistened like a million stars. Her long blonde hair was full of lovely ringlets hanging loosely down around her shoulders. Lying elegantly around her delicate neck was a gold chain made up of a hundred tiny golden leaves. In the middle of this solid Welsh gold necklace, was a platinum figure of Tianaju riding her faithful elk Bellow. Also right there, sitting on her shoulder, was none other than Skittle the squirrel, chewing a nut.

Tianaju's magnificent carriage was carved from the trunk of the largest oak tree in Fairyland. King Drahol had the wheels carved from four limbs taken from the same tree. This tree has no name; it is unique and has always been in Fairyland since time began. It never dies, it just grows back again in three days. Winding around each wheel spokes, were the sweet, fragrant honeysuckle flowers Bellow loved so much. The team driving her special carriage was no other than the great elk's family. There were six in all, four sons and two daughters. Their harness was draped with silver bells shaped like acorns and in front of this heart-warming procession was Bellow's pure white son, Nabalion. He was the image of his proud and mighty father, except for his fabulous white coat and antlers. This handsome son of the princess's hero walked unattached in front of his brothers and sisters. No other elk had ever been graced with such a privilege, and his appreciation of this honour showed in every stride he took. The impressive-looking elk was a truly magnificent sight. And as he walked, his head and antlers moved from side to side while his shiny white coat rippled in the breeze. Flanking the beautiful princess's carriage, were four mounted Royal Guards, all wearing purple coloured uniforms, with shiny gold buttons. Draping gently on the backs of their palomino horses were their long velvet cloaks.

Following the princess, in another glorious carriage was King Drahol and Queen Roaniler, together with Rathier the Fairy Godmother. Tianaju's sister Princess Anoralee and her husband Prince Salown followed next. After them came every Duke, Duchess, Lord and Lady in the world of fairies. Six mounted guards accompanied every stately carriage. All these guards wore their own country colours, and each one held their wands across their chests. The sound of every guards' boots and horses' shoes as they marched through the streets was so intense that everyone cheered with emotion. Hovering above this colourful procession was a choir of a thousand fairies, all singing praises to their beautiful princess.

This wonderful event can only be described as spectacular. To try and describe it in great detail would be impossible. This once in a lifetime event was the first-ever and would never happen again.

When the princess arrived at the impressive Vanbolena Cathedral, the largest in Fairyland, thousands of cheering fairies were waiting for her. "Hail, Princess Tianaju."

Tianaju walked elegantly up the aisle with Skittle still sitting quietly on her shoulder. Her purple cloak flowed magically, wavering as she walked. Following were King Drahol and Queen Roaniler. Behind them, came Princess Anoralee, Prince Salown, the Fairy Godmother and all the other Royals.

At the head of the church, in front of the altar, were three thrones and a golden stand. Tianaju sat in the middle and to her left was the gold stand. King Drahol sat to Tianaju's right; Queen Roaniler sat to her left while Skittle sat on a white silk cushion to the king's right.

The ceremony was performed by the Arch Fairy, Phalujon. It was quite a long ceremony lasting until midnight. Then, at the very stroke of twelve, the great Bell of Wonder, above the Tower Of Life rang out signifying that it was now time for the princess's crowning. Simultaneously, there was a flash of coloured lightning in the Cathedral's entrance leaving a tower of white flames. Tianaju's heart leapt with joy for as the flames disappeared, there standing in the doorway, flickering his snow-white wings, was Etredelmah. With his long wavy, hazel coloured hair falling to his shoulders, he walked up the aisle, towards the princess. Across his chest, he held a pure white wand with a twinkling little star upon its tip. His uniform was two-tone red, his sandals black, laced up to his knees. You could say he looked very similar to a Roman General on parade.

Etredelmah marched up to the beaming princess and bowed to her.

"I have been sent to honour you with great privileges, your Highness."

He then turned to the Cathedral's doors and with his wand, flashed a beam of light towards it. The great doors opened and in flew Sharpy, the glorious buzzard. He was carrying a glistening crown full of sparkling emeralds which he gently placed on the gold stand beside Princess Tianaju.

Etredelmah stepped up to the princess and placed his wand gently upon her head. The moment it touched her, the pure white wand turned a lovely colour green. He then gently rested the glowing wand across the princess's knees.

"This is yours now, Princess Tianaju. It has special magical powers and will glow forever."

He smiled, then after lifting up the twinkling emerald crown, he said while gently placing it on her head.

"Princess Tianaju, with the power given to me, I now crown you the Emerald Queen of Children."

At that point, the cathedral orchestra began to play, joined by a choir of fairies singing the newly written coronation hymn, 'Shadow Mountain,' composed by Petia & Cariluji.

Everyone joined in the singing of the hymn as it echoed around the massive cathedral and all over the wonderful land of Vanbolena.

With the hymn now finished, Etredelmah turned and said to the Emerald Queen of Children.

"Go now in peace, my Queen. Tell all the children throughout the world your once in a lifetime story. To assist you on your travels will be Nabalion, the white son of your faithful friend Bellow. He will be your loyal guard with great powers to fly and carry you anywhere throughout the world. Nabalion will also live forever.

He then pointed to the doors and in came the magnificent white elk, Nabalion. Nabalion walked proudly up to his queen, stretched out his strong front legs and bowed. He then stood up and after looking at her with his lovely amber eyes, turned to the congregation and roared, "Hail, the Emerald Queen of Children."

Hearing this, the congregation erupted with everyone crying out, "Hail, the Emerald Queen of Children."

The beautiful Queen was beaming with delight now and felt very honoured.

"It's time for me to leave you now, my lovely Queen," said Etredelmah. "We'll surely meet again. So until then, I bid you farewell."

He walked slowly away up the long aisle and stopped in front of the grand cathedral doors. Turning now for the last time, he waved to the lovely queen and was gone.

Everyone poured out their loyal love for their newly crowned Emerald Queen of Children by filling the air with sweet hymns and music.

During the last verse of the final hymn, Tianaju, with Skittle on her shoulder, rode her magnificent elk up the aisle and out into the warmest reception anyone could ever wish for. The delighted Emerald Queen of Children, rode along, leading the royal procession back through the city streets of Vanbolena. There were excited fairies everywhere, all of them cheering and singing with tremendous passion.

"Hail Tianaju. The Emerald Queen of Children. The most beautiful fairy in the world."

"I love you. I love you all," said the queen as she waved to the excited fairies.

Back at the castle, Simantrean, the lovely Queen's General, superbly organised the spectacular celebration that went on all night and for six days after. Everyone played sports and games; even the Royal families joined in with the fun. Happiness like this had never been known.

Tianaju is a very understanding and compassionate Queen. She has never married. Instead, she dedicated her life to all the children of the world. The beautiful

Emerald Queen has stayed faithful to her mission. Travelling at bedtime across the globe, telling children her once in a lifetime story. On the night of every full moon, the Queen can be seen travelling like a slow falling star, galloping down the enchanted moonbeams upon her fabulous white elk, Nabalion. Every child that has ever seen the Queen and listened to her story have never been afraid. The lovely Queen is so unbelievably beautiful, they instantly fall in love with her.

I know this to be true for I was one of those children. I was eight years old when the beautiful young, blonde-haired Queen appeared at my bedside. She held my hand and quietly told me her lovely story. Now, I'll tell you mine. It all started that night after the beautiful Queen gave me a lock of her hair…..

Yours truly
Welusa Layovoy

Drahol...Harold

Gormethoda.........................a Godmother

Vanbolena..................................Blaenavon

Roanifer...Lorraine

Rathier..Harriet

Anoralee..Eleanora

Erdelmah...............................The emerald

Pheler...Helper

Nurateth.....................................The lunar

Iwedilli.......................................I will die

Lidapler...All pride

Threedegy...........................The greedy

Rathlie......................................The liar

Aslarili...All liars

Clereman....................................Cruel men

Ohibronoeler............................O horrible one

Mascoedeth................................Death comes

Apsinider..In despair

Hetraleonie...........................Hole in a tree

Tianaju.........Juanita = means the grace of God

Cened Trish................................Christened

Esarapid..Paradise

Nabalion..An albino

Tanyadurew................................Turned away

Simantrean.............................Martin Sean

Petia & Cariluji....................Patricia & Julie

Salown...Lawson

Phalujon....................................John Paul

At the end of the story use a mirror